**MEMORIES ARE MADE C**

**Contents:**

Acknowledgements

Comment by the author

Parts of the book:

    1. So this is me, Alice

    2. My friends and family

    3. Still doing what they do best

    4. That's life

    5. There to help!

    6. From cradle to grave

    7. And so...

Epilogue by the author

**Acknowledgements:**

I would like to thank all those who so willingly gave me their stories for inclusion in the book.

My grateful thanks go to Bev Davies, Catherine O'Mahony, Olive Cottrel, Steve Sexton and Julie Leckey who have done so much to keep me in order! Grateful thanks also must go to Chris Harper for producing the picture of Alice.

As always I would like to thank my husband, Peter, for his patience, tolerance and love - not to mention the hard work he has put into this book.

**Comment by the author**

Old age means different things to different people. When you are very young you think anyone over about 35 is old. Certainly when you get to 55, or more, many people start thinking, somewhat more seriously, about the aging process. Not just the wrinkles and stiff joints, but about the future and what that might hold.

Getting old is something that happens to other people. There is a lot of resistance to the concept of aging, though there is not much one can do about it. There is also a lot of misconception about old age. The approach to aging is one that differs with the individual – do you fight it or succumb? Certainly Alice, the storyteller, is fighting it. It is no wonder though that people fear ageing when all we see in the media are headlines about the loneliness and frailty of old age.

One thing old age does, is make people think about the past. Alice, who is in her eighties, reminisces at times throughout the book. She also recounts the reminiscences of her friends who have revealed their own, often very frank, accounts of their lives.

A recent obituary would seem to sum up Alice:

John Smith, aged 84, died, <u>reluctantly</u>, on June 1st

**Part 1**

**So this is me, Alice**

Today feels like the worst day of my life. They've taken away my freedom. They've said I'm too stupid to drive my car anymore. I am sure they didn't say stupid but that's how it feels. They probably said things like 'Alice, it's in your best interest' or 'with your developing condition Alice,' whatever that means, but to me it feels as though I have had a limb cut off. There are older people than me still driving a car - I'm only in my eighties.

Actually, getting old is something that happens to other people, you still feel the same person inside whatever social and mobility problems you might have. I still like to get dressed up, to wear nice clothes, shoes and coats. I've had to change my colour schemes a bit though since my hair went really grey. I'm also not quite as tall as I was but it hasn't stopped me doing all the things I like doing such as dancing and shopping.

I know someone who went off to Australia on her own to see her family and she was 93 years old. She didn't sit at home moaning, she got on with her life and I suppose that is what I have got to do. Just because I can't drive any more doesn't mean I have got to stop living. In fact, just writing this down has given me an idea. I am going to open a new bank account and put all the money in it from selling my car. I'll also put into this account the money I used to spend on tax, insurance and maintenance as well as petrol. I can then use this money to get a taxi whenever I want. I will stay independent that way and will still be able to have fun.

I've driven since I was in my teens. I used to drive ambulances during the War when we were off duty from nursing. We helped out whenever we could. The ambulances we drove were converted from large saloon cars. The back bodywork was cut off and a canvas cover installed which could be rolled up. The ambulance I drove was an old Buick. Parking it for the first time in the pitch black I discovered it was taller than the shelter and I removed some guttering from the shelter.

When I was the driver I had to check the tyres, radiator and battery every time I drove the ambulance. One day when driving along there were horrible rumbles from the radiator and we ground to a halt. I unscrewed the radiator cap and a jet of sludge flew into the air. Some soldiers who were watching pushed the ambulance back to the depot. It turned out that children had filled the radiator with sand! Another time the ambulance was covered with milk after I collided with a milk cart so I had to clean it before anyone could take it out – ugh, the smell of the stale milk was horrid!

When you have driven for as long as me it's no wonder I don't want to stop driving. I've always loved driving. Charles, my husband, was happy to be driven so whenever we went on holiday or to visit friends and family I always drove. We had some great cars. My first was a little black second hand 1938 Morris 8 that cost me £10 to buy after the War. After we were married I worked as a school nurse part time. Every morning my little car got me to the school which was some 5 miles away in the market town of Sudbury. After about a year it got too expensive to maintain so we took it to the tip and dumped it. I dread to think what it might be worth now but that's how things were in those days.

Next we bought a new Triumph Herald Estate. It was a metallic blue colour and I just loved it, it was speedy and practical. Quite a few years later Charles had an accident whilst driving the Herald, the insurance company wrote off the car. Our next car, a Morris Marina, was a bit boring, even though it had a 'souped-up' engine. I did prefer the Herald.

Charles was always such a smart person – polished shoes, brushed hair, neatly creased trousers and collar and tie no matter where we were going. Although he didn't drive much he looked after the cars, much as he looked after himself. They were always sparklingly clean inside and out. I guess that was probably because of his military training.

Charles then had an accident in the car. Although he didn't seem badly hurt by the accident, he never quite recovered. He started getting bad headaches which meant he couldn't always get to work. For quite a few years the company was very good – Charles had left the RAF after the War and was doing research and development for an electronics company. However, as his time in work became less and less and his time at home more and more they started to make suggestions about him retiring early. This was in 1972. There was a recession on because of the oil crisis.

Poor Charles, when he stopped work after his forced retirement he started to be depressed; as well as having headaches Charles let his appearance deteriorate. He didn't care about his looks the way he had in the past. Life was pretty glum – no job for Charles, not much money coming in, Patsy, my daughter, had left home, firstly to go to college and then she got married to this dreadful chap. I am pretty sure why she married him, it was purely for sex. In those days people used to want to be a virgin until after they were married and I know she had inherited my strong sex drive. Anyway, she had married Brian by the time she was 20 and had divorced him by the time she was 25 having had a baby in the meantime. My granddaughter Jane has 3 lovely children, Joe, Molly and Sam. They are the loves of my life though I don't see them as much as I would like as they are always so busy.

The trouble with getting old is it's hard to concentrate on one thing at a time. I was thinking about how I was going to cope having been forbidden to drive and the next thing I am thinking about is some of the cars we had.

Anyway, my friend, Norman, challenged the decision to stop me driving. He thought I could drive. Not far, mind, but just to the shops or to my club or even to the doctors! As he wasn't family no-one would listen so it looks as though I won't be able to carry on driving after all.

I can't bear the thought of having to get someone to take me everywhere. Imagine having to get a taxi just to visit a friend. Thinking about it seriously, though, perhaps there should be a compulsory driving test for anyone over 70 years of age which should be re-taken say every 3 years. This should help to ensure totally unfit people are not driving around and it will take the pressure off families who think their relative shouldn't be driving.

Of course, Patsy agrees with the doctor. She thinks I'm unsafe on the road. She says she worries when I am out in the car. And anyway, what about the safety of other people? Patsy always was so sensible; so practical I don't know where she gets it from! She even wears sensible clothes, no frills, no bright colours, just white or black or brown and sensible shoes. She often buys her clothes from charity shops. Although we are both tall and fairly solidly built that is about as much as my daughter and I have in common. I love getting dressed up to go out, love buying new clothes and ooh shoes, I adore them! I think I must have 100 pairs!

Patsy doesn't dye her hair or have it cut in a nice modern style. It is just plain. Until I was about 80 I was always changing the colour of my hair but now I have decided to 'grow old gracefully' – at least as far as my hair is concerned – so I am now quite grey, almost white.

The next thing Patsy will want is for me to go into one of those dreadful old people's homes – 'for the best' I am sure she will say. My friend Brenda Jones' family put her into a home. It's a home especially for those with Dementia and Alzheimer's. There really are some strange people there and Brenda seems so much brighter and more alert than the rest of the residents. It seems such a shame. Brenda's wish, for as long as I have known her, was that she should die in her own home and now she won't.

Brenda (Bren) was just the opposite of Patsy. She always spent a lot of money on beautiful clothes, lovely scarves and exquisite jewellery. Even when I visit her in the home she looks so nice - much better than the other residents who seem to have been put in any old rag bag of clothes that happen to be around. When she knew she was going into the home she even bought herself some new, very expensive, spectacles. Anyway, Bren had a nasty fall and had to go into hospital as she had broken a bone. When she was due out she couldn't go home as her house was deemed unsafe by social services. Her silly son had not had any maintenance done on the house for years so he had to have the wiring re-done and a new boiler installed. Whilst this was happening Brenda went into a home. I thought at the time, that's just what the family wanted. And I was right. The next 'phone call I had was from the daughter-in-law, saying that Brenda was in a home for people with Alzheimer's. She would be there for the rest of her days. Poor old Bren. The only saving grace is that the home doesn't smell of urine - not like some of the homes I've visited.

Bren really isn't that bad mentally and whenever I go to visit her she always asks about when she is going home. That has just made me feel worse about not being able to drive; I won't be able to visit Bren. I can't imagine Patsy would take me. It's no good, I'll just have to get used to the idea of taking a taxi everywhere.

## So this is me, Alice

When I visited her recently she couldn't find her spectacles so I asked the nurse if she had seen them. She took us to a room where there were over 50 pairs in a drawer. Bren insisted that none of them were hers so an urgent call was made to the opticians for a new pair. When they arrived they were identical to the pair in lost property but Bren, had, of course, forgotten what the new pair looked like!

Bren and I had such fun when she was well. I remember one time she told me that I was developing a 'widow's hump' – my back was becoming rounded. She said I should regularly lay on the floor with my back hard to the ground. A great idea, I thought, until I tried to get up! Eventually I crawled to the side of the room and managed to pull myself up on the chair. I never did that again but do try to keep my shoulders back. It still makes me laugh when I think of me stuck on the floor.

There seems to be something psychological about 65. Things start to go wrong with your body, hair and even your teeth. The dentist just smiles when I need another filling and says 'old age' though I bet she is laughing all the way to the bank! I have also seen a growth in hairs everywhere from pubic hairs, hairs on moles, hairs up my nose. I seem to spend so much time getting rid of them! It reminds me of my auntie. She had hairs on a mole on her face and when I was a child I hated being made to kiss her. My mother said auntie couldn't get rid of the hairs as they would grow again. I know differently now. Men too seem to grow hairs in all sorts of funny places even when they don't have hair on their head! I hate hairs, ugh!

I remember being 65. People started saying things like 'Do you think you should...?' Or 'At your age' or someone once said 'That was very good for someone of your age' and even 'You look very well for your age'. For the life of me I can't see what age has got to do with anything. If I want to go to my exercise classes and get hot and sweaty then so be it; if I want to have perhaps one or two too many glasses of wine, so what?; if I want to ride my bike or dance and sing, so what? A GP I know says that you are not old until you are 79 now so why is there so much fuss about being 65 or 70?

Someone said recently that I was becoming dull. Can you believe it? Me who was always life and soul of the party? So I went out and bought a bright yellow jumper and consciously tried to smile and laugh a bit more. They were probably right but it came as quite a shock as I hadn't realised how much I had changed.

One thing I do know has changed is my memory. I used to carry everything in my head - shopping, diary, birthdays, visits; you name it I always remembered it. Now, I have to write everything down. Sometimes I even go to the shops for a specific item, buy lots of other things and then find I have forgotten to buy the very thing I went into the shop for in the first place. They say that as we age our long term memory improves and our short term memory deteriorates and that certainly applies to me. I remember things from way back I didn't even know I knew, yet I can't remember to switch the oven on in time to cook a meal. I now have post-it notes all over the house reminding me to do something or to buy something. I even put one on my pillow in the morning so I remember to take my tablets in the evening.

The husband of my next door neighbour bought her a Porsche for her 50th birthday. It looked great and I was really pleased when she offered to take me to choir practice in it. Great ride, fabulous acceleration, comfy seats; everything was fine until I needed to get out! My legs were so stiff it was such an effort and I then had to struggle again when we went home.

Talking of choir, I'm surprised I haven't mentioned Rock Choir before. I only joined about 3 years ago but it has really been fabulous. I'm pretty sure I'm the oldest person there but I do enjoy it. There are no scary auditions. You just turn up and they listen to your speaking voice – unless you know which pitch of voice you have – and then they suggest you sing with that group, in my case upper bass. We have such fun and I've made lots of new friends not to mention singing in places I never even imagined visiting. We've sung at the O2 arena, Wembley stadium, the Etihad stadium, Gunwharf to name a few. We have also broken 2 records and are in the Guinness Book of Records. We also went to Abbey Road studios to make a recording.

I've just seen a video clip on Twitter from Australia where some older people, including over 80's have set up a group to perform Pharrell's 'Happy'. They had uniforms, actions and singing. It looked great fun and much better for them than sitting around all day.

I think men change a lot more than women once they reach 70. I am not sure whether it is the 'macho' image men always had of themselves but certainly they don't seem to like the idea of getting old; of not being able to do all the things they used to do; of having a reduced libido; even the men who managed to keep their hair find it has turned grey. Men seem to get somewhat aggressive; certainly they moan a lot more than they did; they often don't want to go out with friends or meet family. Take Lesley, for example, her husband will hardly go anywhere now. Lesley finds this particularly distressing as they were always such a gregarious couple. In fact, she has now decided to go anywhere if she is invited. She says she'll go mad just staying at home and her husband doesn't seem to mind as long as he doesn't have to join her.

Anyway, back to Charles.

*If there hadn't been a War I would never have met him. I think I was fifteen when the War began. I had wanted to be a nurse all my life. I found a cottage hospital called Henry Brock hospital in Scotland. It was a mansion turned into a thirty bedded small surgery with one sister, one matron and the rest young girls wanting to be nurses. I had a very happy two years there, meeting up with a few soldiers who were in barracks in Loch Lomond.*

*The first of the War I can remember was when Clyde Bank was bombed and we got a lot of the patients who were injured. The injured were more or less all from the Gorbles area. We had to de-lice a lot of the women and clean them up. Then my father died and I wanted to be nearer home*

# So this is me, Alice

*so I went to Dundee Royal hospital. I had one day a month off and worked a ten hour day solid. Our only relief was going to the Palais de Dance and meeting up with the Yanks. After the dances I would be pushed over the wall of the hospital by the Yanks as we were meant to be in by 10pm. We would creep up the back stairs then climb up a drainpipe as our room was three floors up. Everyone talked about attempted burglary, but it was us! It was a very hard life but we made our own fun.*

*The Yanks' reputation was that they were over sexed and over paid and over here. I kept company with a sergeant, named Hank. He didn't lay a hand on me. Another was an officer called Bill and he was a nice guy. I said cheerio on the train and when I got back upstairs my room was full of yellow chrysanthemums from him. Going out with the Americans was a bit of relief from our hard work. On another occasion my friend, Joan and I were in a café. Some Yanks were making eyes at us and we ended up going to the pictures with them. They paid for us. They then wanted to go for a stroll in the park. I was not happy with that so we took to our heels and ran off with them chasing us. We managed to just outrun them and we got to the boarding house, where we were staying, by then.*

*Towards the end of the War in Britain I did my midwifery course. I went to Perth to be near my mother. I did six months instead of a year – part practice. After that I joined the Queen Alexandra's nursing service (QAINS) as a sister in York in a field hospital for six months. I was involved in a lot of brain surgery in York and from there we were shipped out to Udine, Italy, for about six months and then transferred to the hospital in Trieste where I met Charles in 1944.*

*There was an RAF officers' mess in Trieste and they invited us to a party. That was the first time I had experienced any alcoholic drinking. I wasn't used to it. I drank gin which I didn't like much and then we had cherry brandy. I threw the whole lot up in the toilet so didn't drink either again!*

*We had the use of a nice swimming pool when we were in Trieste. As a nursing sister we were ranked as a lieutenant so we could use all of the officers' facilities. We were often collected by a jeep. An RAF chap brought us to the swimming pool in the jeep. When he went to take us back the jeep had been stolen. This often happened or sometimes the wheels were taken off.*

*All the nurses and orderlies we worked with in Italy were Italian civilians. The male orderlies were very good but you had to show them how to work. They would do it if you did it, but you had to do it with them. In the maternity ward there were nursing sisters and Italian midwives. I could practise midwifery as there were other doctors with me.*

*Italy was still occupied. We worked in a military hospital mostly treating British patients, some still injured from the War, some serious accidents. I remember a really bad accident. I was the only sister on duty, the rest were orderlies. A soldier rang me and told me about the accident. At the time I was in the maternity theatre looking after a lady in labour. I remember leaving her with a well experienced Italian midwife while I went down to deal*

## So this is me, Alice

*with the accident. The next day, I was brought in front of the matron and questioned about having left the woman in the middle of her labour with an Italian midwife. I was really on the carpet about this. Eventually the matron took me in front of the colonel. I said I felt it was more important for me to go to sort out the accident when the lady was in the care of a well qualified midwife. Later I went back to the labour ward where the lady eventually produced a baby boy when I was there. The colonel was very pleased but didn't show it - he was pleased I had attended to the lads. He didn't give me a dressing down, took no action in fact. Matron was very small and I think she didn't like me as I was tall. We were all given mess money to buy food. Matron did the shopping and she always bought things I didn't like.*

*I had many boy friends, but they were just friends. One particular boy thought I was serious but I wasn't. One married guy took me out and I thought I was safe! Victor Sylvester, the famous bandleader, was a captain in the army and he ran the entertainment for the troops. People sent him requests. One of the requests was "There was I waiting at the church". This was meant to be for me to have a laugh at because I preferred to go out with this married man. Then there was another one "Oh you beautiful doll" - this was from the orderlies and patients from one of my wards. Life was very hard but a lot of fun.*

*In Dundee I earned £7.50 a month. In the army it was £21 a fortnight, of which I sent home £3 to my mum. We went on duty at 8am and off duty at 6pm.*

*We were invited to lots of cocktail parties on ships that came into port. Four of us always put our names down. The matron wanted us to let someone else go but there were no others so we ignored her and went anyway. That is how I met my husband, Charles. I had gone on board with a marine captain. Later, we all went off the ship to drink and dance at the Otto Club, which was an officers' club. I was dancing away when I was tapped on the shoulder by this really handsome guy. I was a little tipsy, so didn't take much notice of the guy with whom I was dancing. The next day my friend said that someone would like to have a date. I said I can't remember who it was but I went out with him for dinner, then to the officers' club and had a dance.*

*After that, he took me out every day. Not only was he handsome, he was so funny. We seemed to have the same sense of humour so laughed at the same things. He also seemed very kind, thoughtful and gentle. I just enjoyed his company so much better than anyone else I had ever met. On the Wednesday we went to the officers' club for tea. He had brought all his family photos with him. I wondered what was going on. He said his ship was sailing on the Sunday. On the Saturday he asked me to marry him. I said yes, as I had fallen completely in love. We didn't see each other for another three months, until the ship came in again.*

*I took a week's leave and we went to Venice on a bus. Oh, we had such fun! We stayed in the Danielle hotel, it was an officers' hotel and we paid 9d per day for which we were also fed. Now it is the best hotel in Venice. We had separate rooms with four-poster beds. At that time the borders were closed between Yugoslavia and Italy. After our stay in Venice we had to get back to Trieste. There was a border control so the soldiers asked for our passes. We didn't have any but showed them our meal tickets, they obviously couldn't read English so let us through.*

*As soon as we were both posted back to England we got married. I wasn't pregnant or anything it was just that was the way of things during the War. The uncertainty of everything made waiting for anything seem silly. We were so happily married. When Charles died I was devastated. It was so difficult afterwards as Charles had done everything for me – he was so wonderful. He had paid all the bills and managed the money, organised our holidays, got the decorator in, yes, he did just about everything. Suddenly I was on my own and it was really hard. A few times I am sure I have been tricked but I wouldn't tell anyone as they would think I was stupid, which I am not, it's just that I was not used to doing all these things......
Thinking about it now, it's probably why I spend so much money on clothes and shoes – Charles was so careful with money.*

----ooOoo----

Eventually, sometime after Charles' death, I decided to make some changes in my life. I got a part-time job at Southampton School of Nursing. I really loved it there. I got to meet lots of new people and the students were so lovely. At about this time I met Eddie at the bridge club who became the love of my life. Now I've got this friend Norman. Norman's very nice if a little boring. I said after Eddie died I wouldn't get emotionally involved again and I haven't really. Norman and I go out to the cinema together and occasionally we cook each other meals but he never stays over. Patsy says he is bossy and she is probably right but I don't seem to mind. It's pretty good having someone to make decisions.

As you get older you want company; you want someone to talk to and listen to your views but certainly I have this feeling of wanting to be on my own and to making my own mind up, hard as that might be, so Norman and my relationship is ideal for me now. As you get older you also remember things in your life you thought you had forgotten (or would prefer to forget). It's good to write it down so it's not forgotten and you can leave it for your nearest and dearest.

**Part 2**

**My Friends and Family**

"*I'm going upstairs to sort out the washing,*" said Pat to her husband "*whilst you check the lottery tickets". I heard him call out several times, not very loud mind, so didn't think anything of it. I carried on with the washing. When I came downstairs he was on the floor – he'd had a heart attack. Oh what a conscience I had. The trouble with being married to someone for so long is you get to know, or think you know, what they will do and how they will behave. Oh how wrong I was in this case. Luckily we got him to the hospital in time for them to treat him. He's pretty good now fortunately.*" – extract from an e mail from Pat.

---ooOoo---

Families do funny things. There is a saying that 'You can choose your friends but not your family'. This is so true in so many circumstances. How many times do you go to a family party for example only to find there is no-one there you have the least bit in common with? Or how many times do Christmases land up as slanging matches as some relative has said something that has upset someone else?

It's also true that the way we are bought up, either deliberately or accidentally, can have a long term effect with how we are as people especially as we get older.

One of the things that annoys me about getting old is that it seems that everyone wants a bit of a say about what I should be doing; where I should be going; how I should be saving/spending my money. Most people have to trust their family if they have one, or their friends, when they become unable to care or make decisions for themselves. This happened to Sharon, who gave her youngest son the power to manage all her financial affairs. Unfortunately, the family have learned now that he was not an honest person and has taken a lot of Sharon's money. She died almost destitute. How could he? He was so clever it looks as though the police are not going to prosecute. Not only does it seem as though he has got away with it but the rest of the family are not going to receive the inheritance to which they were entitled.

In old age, families take on different perspectives and different levels of importance. Different families have different ideas of their role. A woman who works in our local post office thought that she should look after her mother through thick and thin. Her mother has been cantankerous all her life. She was always moaning or complaining about something. As she got older, probably into her early 80's, she started to spend more and more time living at her daughter's home until eventually she moved in permanently. Her daughter and the rest of the family made all sorts of provisions for her so she was comfortable and well cared for but still she moaned.

Her mother then started showing signs of dementia and became unwell too. She went into hospital and then into a nursing home. However, the daughter was not happy about her mother being in a home and decided that she could come back to her house - very laudable but the trouble she is causing doesn't bear thinking about. She doesn't want the carers who come in every day to look after her; she insists her daughter or granddaughter do everything. She refuses to be lifted by a hoist into and out of the bath; sometimes she totally refuses to eat or complains about the quality of the food and so on and so on. Her family's life is absolutely hell. Personally, I don't see why they didn't put her into a home. She has a house to sell so it is not as though the family need to be out of pocket.

In some cultures it is true that families stay together and support their elders. Some say it is their religion that dictates how they behave towards older people but surely it is to do with the relationship of the person and their family. I would hate to think that my family think I expect them to look after me when (if) I become a pain in the butt! I think we should write down what we feel we would want when we are no longer able to care for ourselves. I have a friend whose father thought his son should attend to his every need for the rest of his life after his wife died. Suddenly the old chap decided he wanted to go into a nursing home – aged 89. After a few weeks, he decided he wanted to go back to his own flat, he didn't like the constraints of the home. A complete care package was set up which lasted all of 6 months when he decided that a care home was after all the best for him but not before he had accused his carers of taking his money and his son of not visiting often enough. It was almost a no-win situation for everyone involved.

A win-win situation was Lucy's case. However, she was much younger, only 66, when she became widowed..... She told me:

*My husband died in 2004 and a couple of years later after the children had left home I began looking for a male companion who would go to the theatre, out for dinner and go on cinema trips. I had a single friend who used a website called 'Make friends on line' and she suggested that I give it a go. I didn't have much luck to start with. I needed a new life but, at that time, I didn't want a partner.*

*This site gives you the opportunity to set out your profile in lots of detail and the search engine scores on points. It recommends matches with people with similar interests. Gerry came up as new client. I did like his picture but I didn't do anything about it. However his photo kept coming up and eventually I sent a message to him through the service asking if he would like me as a contact. He lived a long way away which was probably a good thing, because there was no commitment to being close to each other. I felt safer as I wouldn't just bump into him in my local patch.*

*In fact we didn't meet at first. We started an e mail correspondence for about a year. He was witty, he made me laugh and at the time he was dealing with some problems with family relationships and we used each other as a confidant. The fact that we didn't meet made it more honest; it all came out in the wash. You can say things in an e mail that you wouldn't say face to face.*

*I think that we just let the relationship grow. I grew to trust him on his word. After the third e mail, I decided to wait a few days before I replied. He sent a message 'A good man could die of thirst waiting for a reply from you!' All our e mails were written late in the evening about 11ish as that's when we sat down - because we were living our lives during the day. It's at about that time that sometimes things overwhelm you and you need someone to chat to; sharing each other's troubles.*

*I had been extremely happily married; it was a very good marriage. We were a brilliant team; we worked together building up a company. It was very hard to let go when my husband died. It was within 6 weeks of hearing the prognosis that he died. When I got to know Gerry via e mail, it was a life saver. I felt 'I could dump that stuff' when I had someone with whom I could share it. My family had been fantastic and supportive but Gerry had something else to offer. Our lives were in parallel. He was on his own. He had brought two children up from ages 12 and 14 after his wife left. His mother had died in 2004. He lost a very good career because of an aggressive takeover so he was traumatised by all of that. When we started communicating our kids had grown up and they were moving on. We had a lot of shared grief.*

*Gerry is reliable, trusting and he made me laugh. I don't know how it happened but one day we mentioned talking to each other on the phone. I didn't want that because the e mails were so lovely and I thought it might spoil or maybe end our relationship but it kind of creeps up on you and we decided to speak to each other on the phone. He had a lovely voice. We didn't swap pictures after the initial registering photo but you build up an idea of what the person looks like. I knew his height etc, so I had a rough idea of how he looked. We had phone contact for a little while and then there was the suggestion we should meet. I found it difficult to move on but we did. We met on neutral territory; I was so cautious. I warned my girlfriend to expect a phone call from me 10 minutes afterwards. We met at Hindhead. I phoned her and said 'He's alright'. He was there already but as he came towards me I knew him. It was instant. I needed a man and he was that man. It was not long after that we spent weekends together and then progressed into 'we'll move in together'.*

*He put his house on the market. He was going to move in with me but the market was very volatile too so he advised that I sell my house as well. Mine sold in 7 days and then his sold and we moved into a rented property. We sold on a high and then we had to think what we were going to do. We were both equally balanced financially so we then decided to look for a property in Cornwall. That didn't work out, the people weren't coping with the way prices were dropping and we eventually found this place where we live now.*

*Alongside all of that was the family. Although people knew – my sister and mother – I was available, it was a bit of a shock to them to realise I had met someone else. So we had a meeting of all my family and then we met Gerry's family. He didn't have many. My sister was the hardest one; my mum fell in love with him. But my sister was incredibly suspicious. She thought he was after my money and his family felt the same about me but we soon got to know the families and it has all worked out. We were honest with everyone and my sister is now Gerry's best friend. My family all confide in him and I am accepted by his family. You have to be very careful with people's sensibilities.*

*We have both been incredibly lucky to have a romance late in life - a full on love experience. You behave with everyone else as normal but this is going on in your life at the same time. He is so honest, decent and a good man. It is a totally different relationship from my first husband who was a driven, volatile, aggressive, and a lovely man who was very determined to succeed. It worked well when we were younger. This is nothing like that now. No competition. It's so different.*

*I did have a very good girl friend - I once travelled to New Zealand with her - who was very supportive when my husband died. However, when I told her the relationship with Gerry was serious she dropped me. She had been dating lots of people without success so it may be jealousy. She genuinely cut me out which was a shame.*

*Gerry and I keep our lives separately in terms of finance. We won't get married ever. We just keep things separate. We don't need to get married. When you are younger you need the reinforcement – grow up, have family etc. We have a legal tie up so we know where we stand, what is joint etc and we both wrote a new will. When you are older you have to be much more calculating; aware; conscious of others, and of the consequences of your actions. You have to 'cross the T's and dot the I's' including discussing death, what you are going to do. You also need to be more practical, know what you need, negotiate your own space. I have my own room/office which is important to me.*

Internet dating has become a real 'must have' as far as I can see. Everyone is talking about it. Apparently, 60% of all those using internet dating are over 50. Do you know that there are even dating sites for the over 80's? I didn't believe it but when I went onto the internet I saw that it was true. I guess that if you are over 80 the dating companies think you don't have long to live so dates need to be organised pretty quickly, that's why, in addition to normal terms, the companies offer speed dating in sheltered housing and tea dances where the over 80's can meet and act pretty quickly. I can't stop giggling about this. Can you imagine someone on their Zimmer frame trying to hurry to the next chair or someone needing to go the loo and not wanting to miss their turn? The mind boggles!

There seems to be hundreds of sites catering for over 70's. They even give tips on going on dates – often the person's first date, for many, for over 50 years. For men, they say, no hairs in ears or nose or sticking out from eyebrows – definitely a turn-off – ugh the thought turns me off just thinking about it; no medallions or shirts open at the front exposing hairy (grey) chests; clean well groomed clothes that suit the person and are not the height of fashion, plus clean fresh breath. The last sentence also applies to women though they are also told to not wear flat shoes as men of that generation prefer women in heels which must not be so high that the woman can't walk properly. However, apparently, the biggest turn off, for men, is lipstick on teeth (advice given on how to avoid this) and hair roots that are a different colour to the women's hair! Behaviour is also discussed including agreeing on who should pay for things.

Some of my friends have tried these sites. Sometimes we have quite a giggle when they tell us their stories. One person I know whilst on a date couldn't understand what the guy had in his carrier bag. Eventually she asked him. Can you guess? It was a hot water bottle as he found trains rather chilly! One friend said that the photograph his date had put on the site must have been taken years ago as she didn't look anything like that in reality – more like an old prune! I could go on all day telling these stories.

Thinking of dating, reminds me of Eddie. It is really hard after you partner dies. Lots of people offer help and advice at first and then that gradually tapers off. It was ages before I started to do anything for myself after Charles' death, but eventually I decided to join a bridge club at the local centre. I'd learnt to play bridge when we were in Italy during the War. It was amazing. I made lots of new friends at the club and then I met Eddie. He was a widower so we had lots in common. Eddie loved ballroom dancing and asked me to join him at the dance studios where he went. It was fantastic. I had an excuse to get dressed up and Eddie was such a gentleman he made my heart flutter with his compliments and little presents. He was also a really 'snazzy' dresser which I like. When we danced it was as though we had been made for each other. He used to take me home right to my door, give me a little kiss on the cheek, and say goodnight and go.

He had done very well for himself as he had come from a very different background to me but had worked his way up at work and had a really important job when we first met.

Can you believe that Eddie's parents didn't know what the 11+ exam was? They asked him if he wanted to take the exam after receiving a card saying he was eligible. Eddie asked what the options were, they didn't really know except that he would get time off school to do the exam so he said yes. Later, they then got a similar card in another colour telling them he had passed. Again they asked if he wanted to go to a different school from his friends and he said 'Yes.' When he went down to the end of the road where he lived his friends were there. Eddie told them he had passed the 11+ exam. They said they expected their results would come soon which they didn't, however, Bill Brown, one of the lads who was expected to pass the exam eventually became a millionaire. I wonder if he would have become a millionaire if he had passed the 11+?

There is so much emphasis on education of children from such a young age nowadays, I really wonder whether it is worth it. Parents seem to pay for cramming/private tuition. They even leave themselves short of money sometimes just so the child can get a so called better education than they received.

I've wandered off again! But, anyway, the night I invited Eddie in for coffee changed my life for ever! We sat on the sofa chatting for ages about all sorts of things. We seemed to have so much in common. Before I knew where I was we were having sex on my bed – yes the same bed as my husband and I used to sleep on. Oh it was wonderful. I don't remember having sex like that before. Well things progressed very rapidly from there and it wasn't long before Eddie moved in with me. The sex was always fantastic. It didn't matter what time of day or night it was, if we felt like having sex we did. We tried all sorts of different ways, things I had never tried with my husband. We still went dancing regularly but I always had a big smile on my face looking forward to what I knew would be coming next.

However, I made a bit of a mistake one day. I told Patsy what a wonderful sex life I had with Eddie and said it was much better than I had ever had with her dad. Instead of being pleased she was most upset. She said I was undermining her father. In fact, she said, the noise from our sex life had been upsetting her for quite a while. I had no idea she had heard a thing. We had quite a row and eventually it was decided that, for the best, we should sell the large house we were all living in by then – it had been separated into two apartments. It was really sad to leave the place – it was an old converted bakery and I had loved it there. My son-in-law, Patsy's second husband, had done all the building work himself. But life must go on, so Eddie and I bought an apartment together after Eddie sold his bungalow. We were very happy in our own, I guess now, selfish way.

As they say, all good things come to an end and after about 4 years Eddie got cancer. I nursed him for 6 months before he died but even as he was dying he still had that twinkle in his eye!

# Memories are made of this

I was sitting here feeling sorry for myself even though I know there are people much worse off than me. The postman has just called and I have a letter. It's ages since I had a proper letter. It's so nice to get a real letter. This one is from a friend called Do whom I met during the War. She is over 90 and her family put her in a home a year or so ago. She is so bored. She says that all the residents do is eat and sleep. The staff encourage Do to play bingo. Can I imagine Do playing bingo? I think not.

Anyway, in order to keep her mind busy, she has started to write her life story down – all by hand as she hasn't got round to using a computer. So I made myself a cup of coffee and sat down to read the letter. Do was so full of fun, probably no more than 4ft 10inches tall, always elegantly dressed with huge high heel shoes. Even in her nineties she was always laughing and enjoying life. People used to smile when we went out together and call us 'Mutt and Jeff' after one large and one small comedian.....

*My dearest Alice*

*I wonder if you would be a sweetie and read this for me? I know I can trust you. I don't want my family to see it until after I die so please do keep it to yourself.*

*My father was in the regular army and was commissioned during the First World War. He was given a top honour from France for outstanding bravery. I'm told that he was in the trenches, on the front line from the beginning of*

## My friends and family

*WW1. He originally had brown hair but by the end of the War his hair was totally white.*

*He remained in the army until he was 41 when he retired and took the post office and shop at Nutbourne. He had commuted his army pension in 1922 to buy the post office so money was very tight. I was my parents' little surprise! They hadn't bargained on another child as my brothers and sisters were much older than me. In fact, my eldest sister was 18 years older so they were amazed when I was born at the post office when my mother was 40 on 10th April 1920. Dad lost a lot of money in the shop and post office – bad debts; people didn't or couldn't pay up, together with his lack of experience - so that's why he decided to go to the Sudan after father joined the Colonial Service.*

*My earliest memories are in the Sudan. Mummy and I were pioneers. We went out there to join my father. He had gone to the Sudan 3 months before to get settled. He was an engineer in charge of the telephone system from Atbara to Khartoum. It was British; General Gordon was then murdered. Later Sudan went back to the Sudanese.*

*I came back to England when I was 7 as they thought I should go to school. I hadn't been to school before as my mother had taught me. I am told that I was well ahead of anyone in the UK. Mummy and daddy went back to Khartoum. That was the last time I saw my father. My sister looked after me. My father died of dysentery. He went into hospital in Khartoum and 3 days later he was dead. My mother had to come back to England alone.*

*Life was very different then. I no longer had black people to look after me nor was I able to do what I wanted. All my friends had been Arab girls and boys. I came back and went to a sweet little prep school in Chichester called St Margaret's as my sister lived in Chichester. I had to wear gaiters with a button hook. I lived opposite a farm with my sister and her family. There were 2 daughters on the farm and I have very happy memories of the farmer's wife. She was always cooking lots of cakes which we would take through the fields to the men who were harvesting.*

*They were happy days when my mother came back and we both lived with my sister. Then mother decided to sink her savings in a house – my father would have had to be in the Sudan for another 7 years before he would have got a pension.*

*Mother and I then lived in our house in Worthing where my mother did bed and breakfast (B&B). When I think about it, I don't know how she managed but she just had to get on with it. She had never been short of money all her life, so it was a real struggle for her. In the summer we went back to live with my sister whilst we let out the whole house. An agent absconded with our money and other people's money too. Mother decided to sell the house and took a furnished flat in Chichester. She used to do night nursing. I was left on my own but there were other people in the block of flats.*

*In 1939 I was 17 and a trainee manager for the Maypole Dairy. The men were being called up. Mother said "If you stay at the dairy you will be in a reserved occupation so* you won't get called up." I started doing that but more than anything I really wanted to join up. Then we saw a big house to let. If we could furnish that, my mother said, that would be an income. So we took it. I had some money left to me by my grandmother which I couldn't touch until I was 21 so we asked the executor if we could have an advance which we did. We were running that as a B&B when the War started.

*Soon after the War began I became restless. After about 6 months the War was well underway and I really wanted to join the air force – I came from a military family. Mother was not happy but my elder sister persuaded her to let me sign on.*

*I joined the WAAF. I trained as a radio telephone operator, taking over from the men. I later became a corporal and had nearly 4 years in the air force where I met many interesting people and had a wonderful time - the camaraderie and the excitement. Often I had to give bearings based on the information we had in order to put a fix on people so they could be rescued if possible. Life was very 'here today gone tomorrow'. Friends you danced with the night before were gone the next day.*

*I used to hitch to/from Cambridge, where we did our initial training, to London. That was before I went to Canada for flight training. Mainly military personnel picked us up but on one occasion 2 civilians gave us a lift - there were 3 of us. I never hitched alone. They called us faith, hope and charity.*

*My pay when I joined was 22 shillings per fortnight. There was initial training of 'square bashing' for 3 weeks and then 3/4 months training. I had to have a certain knowledge of physics and then I was sent to the signals section of the air force.*

*Once I went back to see my mother. She thought I wasn't fed, though we had wonderful food during the War. I was stationed at RAF Debden in Saffron Walden by then. I left mummy in Chichester to go back to London and meant to meet my watch but no-one was there because of the bombings. The air training officer (ATO) who was liaising between the forces spoke to me. He said, "There is a late train to Saffron Walden with blue lights. The train is full of soldiers - half of them merry!" I got on that train and then got off at Audley End as Saffron Walden was a Quaker station and there were no trains on Sundays. I had to go 3 miles with a case full of goodies my mother had given me. It was now 2 o'clock in the morning. Three chaps got off the train and I thought "I hope they won't speak." Then one of them said:*

*"Where are you off to?" to which I replied,*
*"I am stationed in Saffron Walden in private digs."*
*"Do you know what time it is? It is 2 o'clock."*
*One chap said. "I wouldn't want my sister to be out on her own".*

*So he walked me back to my lodgings and I said goodbye to him. I never saw him again. I was really frightened but he was so kind. That was one of my best experiences of the War.*

*I was then posted to Dover which was completely fortified. You can visit it now. We were about 60 foot under the ground. The place had been dug out by the 'non fit for duty' men. There was a complete navy, army and air force under the cliff. We used to get showered there. I was in the Connaught barracks. The old barracks had been bombed but some had been done up so there was a section for WAAF and a section for ATS. I even talked to Winston Churchill. He came to Dover when I was there at the combined headquarters. The combined operations group was one of Churchill's better ideas. It was the first time that all the services actually worked closely together and were stationed together.*

*On a clear day we could see, through binoculars, the patrols of the Germans in France. Then we would hear two air raid warnings which meant we were being shelled. The first intimation of shelling was in the harbour. Then everyone had to take shelter because it was under military control. I sheltered under Shakespeare cliffs many times. My claustrophobia was terrible and I wished to be outside. From there I was posted to Tangmere in Sussex. I worked in the Operations (Ops) room. The Ops room was at Bishop Otter College. Everything had to be separated in case of being bombed. From there I was sent to the pylons and transmitters section where we took over from the men and worked at night - we were on watch. The men were needed for other things.*

*I used to speak to the pilots – ground to air. I was always talking to the pilots over the channel. You could speak to them as long as there was no barrier in the air or on the*

*ground. We had to log everything and the book was taken after the raids as they had to check what was said.
During the dawn patrol, the pilots would get bored so they would call us. We would use our code name and they would say nonsense things such as get the breakfast on, bacon and eggs or see you tonight, but we didn't log these things.
I was on duty with one of my friends who had married a Canadian when there was a Mayday call. Her husband, the pilot, had gone down.*

*You have no sense of fear when you are young. Sometimes in the barracks we would get the warning and put our great coats over our pyjamas to go to Fort Burgoyne. There were 3 groups of people - those who took pillows as they were going to sleep; those who were going to make tea or coffee and the card players. I loved playing cards. We would usually be there 2 or 3 hours. After the last shell we waited half an hour before the all clear and then sometimes there would be another warning so we had to stay longer.*

*I can remember dancing in London with an American. He was boasting and bragging. He was very funny and very kind. We were dancing at the Hammersmith Palais. In war time we saw no civilians. There was every nationality, lots of Americans boasting and then suddenly the military police walked in. Half of these Americans shouldn't have been there. Very soon they disappeared – marched off by the military. That would happen quite frequently. There were masses of navy, air force and soldiers in London who shouldn't have been there but poor lads knew they may have been shot and killed the next day.*

*The Americans were completely self-sufficient; they had everything in their canteen. I was with this American and I told him that the British people had coupons but in the military we had almost everything provided. I said I was short of soap. He said "Don't they give you soap?" I said "No." The next day he brought me a huge box of soap which I shared out with my colleagues.*

*I kept my sister back in Chichester in vests and bras. We were allowed 'one on, one off and one in the wash' so I used to ask for more. I was told to go to the kit parade and say 'lost in the laundry'. All our clothes said 'air women for the use of'. Our knickers were 'blackouts and twilights' - blackouts with elastic and thick, and silky ones for the summer. Half the time you spent climbing about and up ladders so blackouts were best.*

*When I first joined I took my own underwear with me. The first time I washed it and hung it out to dry I never saw it again. It had been stolen.*

*The trains were always full of forces, but no-one said anything about their camp because 'walls have ears'. We said nothing about where we were stationed or what we did; nothing.*

*Our pillows were long bolsters full of straw. Every time we went on leave we handed in our bedding and our pillows and then when we came back we got clean and fresh ones. We had striped flannelette pyjamas and the men said, "You have pinched all our nightwear so we have to sleep in nothing." I think what they meant was that our pyjamas looked like men's pyjamas.*

*I thought about taking the commissioning examinations but I enjoyed being in the ranks. There were one or two WAAF officers in the welfare squad and I thought what a miserable life. I didn't want their miserable existence. I was Aircraftwomen 1st class and then a Corporal. By the time I came out I was earning 35 shillings per week which was all spending money. During the War you were also allowed to have your hair done, teeth done as well as uniforms, food and lodgings.*

*I was going to be a sergeant but discovered I was pregnant. The father was an American called Russell Berriman. He was from Mississippi. He was a really nice chap and great fun. When I told my mother that I was pregnant she said she would support me. I stayed home for a while and then went back to barracks but then I had to leave just after VE day because I was pregnant. Everyone had to leave if they were pregnant.*

*My mother and aunt both liked Russell. Unfortunately he was killed, missing presumed dead, just before Rosalynd, my daughter, was born. I wouldn't have married him anyway as I didn't love him but I didn't want to lose Lindy, as we called her. My mother and I decided not to tell anyone about Russell being the father in case the American authorities or Russell's family wanted to take her back to America. With hindsight this may not have been the best thing for Lindy but it seemed the best decision at the time.*

## My friends and family

*At about this time I met Percy Lemm. He was so tall and well-built you couldn't fail to see him in a crowd. I had gone to the Unicorn pub in Chichester where all the forces people used to meet. I guessed I would soon see people I knew. I saw this farmer chap whom I had met when was 14. He gave me a hug and said, "This is my friend Percy Lemm." I knew Percy didn't recognise me though we had met years before.*

*Even though I had left the forces, I never wore civy clothes as you were always better looked after in uniform. I was dancing with Percy – he was a foot taller than me and it was quite funny really as I just came up to his breast pocket. He said, "How long are you home for? Perhaps we could go out for meal or to the flicks." I played it cool, saying, "I must get home." He slipped his card into my pocket which I didn't realise until I got home. I was broke by now and I thought why not. So I said, "If you meant what you said I'm free." So we went and that was it. The rest is history, I eventually married Percy.*

*During the war I had wonderful times, I will never forget them. The intense camaraderie is my most everlasting memory. You would sit on the train and within no time everyone was chatting - that doesn't happen any more!*

*When I was married I wore a black suit with a pretty, frilly, white blouse and black and white hat with ribbons. I was married in the registry office in Chichester because I was a Catholic and Percy was a Protestant. It was 7$^{th}$ March 1947. We had a reception at Bosham Country Club – six of us and then Percy had to go back to the navy.*

*During the War the shops didn't keep many supplies in case of fire so we were given extra money in the forces but we couldn't spend it, so I had it put in the bank. We were allowed £2 extra per week so when I left the air force I received 2 cheques worth about £50 each. I also had £45 gratuity. Percy was a naval reserve and he had £45. He was offered a commission to stay on but he chose not to stay. He had been on minesweepers.*

*Percy came out of the navy and we had to find somewhere to live. We went to put our names on the council list but they said we 'were not the right type'. Percy said, "I have served in the War and so has my wife. I am not asking for anything free." Percy was so cross he said, "Don't ever accept anything from the council." We found a furnished flat.*

*Percy legally adopted Lindy, she is Lindy Lemm. Percy didn't want to consider that Lindy was not his. She adored him. She was 2 years and 9 months old when we married. It was very special. The funny thing was she looks like Percy. I had another child whom we called Graham.*

*I used to have foreign students to stay as paying guests. We also had PEGs (paying English guests). Percy set up as an insurance broker – he had been in insurance before the War. He called the firm, City & County Insurance Brokers. I became his secretary. The big noise from Robert Bradford, a huge company, would ring up and I might be in my bra and pants or something but would answer the phone. They would ask for the motor department for instance. I would put the phone down, wait a minute and change my voice and answer the query. Someone once said they liked my voice and thought I was efficient!*

*We always worked from home. The first house we lived in was rented and furnished and then after a couple of years we bought a big old Victorian house with plenty of rooms for the office. It was in Chichester. There we stayed until we went to Fishborne. As well as running a business, we had 2 PEGs and 2 children plus my mother-in-law who lived with us for about 4 months before she died. I had always wanted to be a nurse so I was happy to take her on.*

*My mother-in-law always saw any visitors in the morning and then by about 1 o'clock would say, "I've had enough dear, I am going to take my teeth out and have a rest." When she died, we stayed. Lyndhurst Lodge really needed money spent on the electricity wiring. The bulbs were always going. One of our PEGs used to slap his leg and say, '"Percy would say, another bloody bulb gone." They used to take a bulb out just to tease him. One of the PEGs was eccentric, he used to collect hats and would come in and sit down at the table with his hat on. I would say that if he sat down with a hat on I would throw it on the fire. "I told you about your bloody hat, I said I would burn it, and I will" and I did! Everyone roared with laughter!*

*Percy carried on working until he was 80 but retired when computers came and took over. I've been on my own now for 27 years. Percy was 16 years older than me. He died at 83. After he died he left me with a good pension but I needed more that's why I carried on taking in PEGs.*

*When I sold my house, the pension people thought I was dead! I moved from my old address and forgot to tell the insurance company. The occupants of my previous house didn't send on the letters so after 3 years I was presumed dead. They were about to cut my pension off until my daughter-in-law contacted them.*

*Before the War if you went out with a boyfriend you took your mother along! How life has changed.*

*My family don't know much about my life so if you think this is OK I will leave it for them to read when I'm gone.*

*Take care,*
*Do.*
*I bet you were surprised to know that Lindy wasn't Percy's child – we all have our own little secret don't we!*

----ooOoo----

Now I have a huge dilemma, I have just heard that Do has died. She was rushed into hospital and died very suddenly aged 94. I don't know whether to ring Graham and tell him now about the letter or to tell Lindy as it's her the letter will really affect. Should I tell them now or wait until after the funeral? Oh I hate making decisions and the older I get the worse I get. Oh golly, I think I'll tell Graham's wife!

As I said, I met Do during the War. Ooh those were the days! The dances they were so much fun. The jokes and laughter all around were probably a cover up for our worries but that's what I remember now, the fun, the camaraderie and the close friendships. The War changed lives forever. Who would have thought I would have met and agreed to marry Charles within days of meeting him? Take Do for example, we've been friends for years. I think it is because you were thrust closely together in almost surreal circumstances not knowing what the future would hold. You learn to trust people; to put your lives on the line for them. Somehow those feelings hardly seem to exist nowadays.

My best friend, June, had been a single mother for years. In fact, I think she was brilliant the way she seemed to dedicate her life to her daughter, Sam. However, when Sam went off to university, June decided she would like to meet someone for company. When she was at my house one day we wrote down all the things she would want from a man. Eventually, after lots of 'yes' and no's' we came up with this list – liked sport, liked music, would want to go to the theatre, liked cooking. In return for the cooking June said she would do the cleaning and ironing. We had a laugh about how she was going to find 'Mr Right' ……and then she met David – who happened to meet her criteria – and to whom she is now married. David's life has been so different from June's life. I've been friends with June for over 45 years and thought she was going barmy when she became involved with David and well, when she decided to get married, we really thought she was losing it! But we've all been proved wrong and 5 years on they are very happy.

As we get older I guess we reflect on our lives rather more than we do when we are young. When something really bad happens, we think what might have been. Similarly when something good happens we think 'if only'. This seems to be true of David who tells his story......

*I would say I am a pretty gregarious person. I love having a good time; I enjoy good food and fine wine; I enjoy nice clothes of good quality and generally like nice things around me; I like to go to different places around the world. Some people would say that I wear my heart on my sleeve. I am not sure exactly what they mean but I certainly do show my emotions both good and bad and say what I feel. I also value friends and family immensely.*

*Recently I have had a couple of serious health scares which have made me think about my past.*

*Before I met June, I had been married twice, had several 'short flings' and been in a fairly long term relationship – a record I am not proud of. However, I have to say that I have never been as happy as I am now, married to June.*

*I was born in Southsea, in March 1947. After I was born my mother was told that she could not have any more children. My father was steeped in the license trade, and his father had been the owner of a couple of pubs. My parents had several pubs in the south. We went to Bournemouth to a new pub. We only lasted there 6 months as we didn't like some of the unsavoury clientele. We had to employ a boxer and wrestler to keep the peace! We then went back to Portsmouth where Dad went to work for Portsmouth City Council. He eventually became Director of*

*Leisure. During this time he booked the Beatles on two occasions to play at the Guildhall and was responsible for organising and providing food for the Queen several times.*

*My schooling was fairly normal. I had two primary schools then went to a secondary school in Portsmouth. I only lasted two weeks - the ritual of having to put your head down the toilet and flush it was too much both for me and for my dad to accept, so I went to Mile End House private school where he had been before me. I then went to a secondary school in Havant because we lived there by now and it was here that I started to enjoy all sorts of sports.*

*I went through to the 6$^{th}$ form but regrettably my love of sport affected my studies as I was more often than not on the playing field rather than in the classroom. I came out of Warblington school with five 'O' levels which were not enough to go to teacher training college. The 3 things I shone at were religious education, English language and sport. At one stage I was thinking of going to theological college, then becoming a clergyman or to St Paul's at Cheltenham to become a sports teacher.*

*After Warblington, I went to evening classes to get more qualifications to enable me to achieve my career ambitions, but by the time I had finished I had already started work and was earning more money than my friends who had been to college. I worked for the Smiths Food Group - Smith's crisps - and eventually became an area sales manager. When I joined Smiths I was very proud to be given, as a merchandiser, a red white and blue striped* van for my duties. I was allowed to take the van home after work. When I was driving it into the garage on the first occasion, I managed to rip the sign off the top of the van which said 'Crispy, Crunchy, Golden Munchy'. This didn't go down too well on my first day!

I then had several jobs all within the sales/sales management field before joining Cockerills in Southsea as a trainee cutting room manager, then manager. Cockerills made children's clothing under the 'Ladybird' label and employed 300 women and 15 men. After about two years, during a tea break with the 15 men, the production control manager asked us all the question, "If you were going to commit suicide how would you do it?" Jokingly, I suggested going up on Portsdown Hill with a bottle of whisky and a piece of rubber tube; drink the whisky and attach the rubber tube to the exhaust pipe through the window and leave the car engine running. Next day, the police arrived to tell us that he had done just that! I attended the Coroner's Court where the coroner commenced by saying, "I understand Mr Whittle that this was your idea." It's an ill wind, but I got his job – the production manager's job, not the Coroners.

I stayed at Cockerills for 4 years but I missed selling so then spent two years as national sales manager for Rigby Built which was an upholstery company based in Portsmouth. Unfortunately death caught up with me again. The managing director's wife died. It soon became evident that she was the brains behind the business. The company began to falter so I looked around for another job.

*My girlfriend at the time (later to become my first wife) and I were courting and I was living with my parents in Southsea. It was her habit, when she stayed over, to creep into my bedroom at night. On one occasion I was alerted to my father turning the lights on in his bedroom and corridor and coming to my bedroom saying, "There's a very good job in the paper tonight David, as manager of a Hargreaves Sports shop in Southsea." My girlfriend, on hearing my father approach had slipped beneath the covers and moulded herself into my body so as to try to be invisible. After discussing the matter for some time he turned the light off and said, "David, we will have another look in the morning. Good night both of you!"*

*Having joined Hargreaves Sports as a shop manager, I was with the company for 24 years and became a director and shareholder. Martin Hargreaves was managing director and the major shareholder. We are still friends to this day. During this time, Martin became chairman of Intersport and I became chairman of the Intersport Marketing Group. I went away on various photographic assignments to exotic countries with models where it was important to gain an element of team work within the group. I would get on a plane with a group of about nine people I had never met before and would try to break the ice a little so that when we got off the plane we would have some form of team cohesion which was often difficult. On one trip, I remember a model who, when eating out during our 14 days, chose the most expensive food rather than what she really wanted – I went ballistic. After our trip, we produced our first catalogue. We had 3½ million catalogues printed which went out with the Sunday papers 8 weeks before Christmas. We did this for 5 years.*

*One of the best business deals I have ever done in my life was after an introduction from hockey friends to two Dutchmen who supplied products to Makro in Europe. At that time the retail price of top grade tennis balls in England was the same price as the trade price in Holland. I managed to sell the Dutchmen a container load of Dunlop and Slazenger tennis balls which I thought would lead to a one off windfall profit. We wanted to make sure we got as many balls in the container as possible so we loaded the crates, then boxes and then individual balls which we pushed into every crevice in the container. We then received the money by transfer before we sent the container. Three days later we had a phone call from Holland thanking us for the delivery and advising us that they had sold all of them and wanted another shipment – but this time not loaded as before. We hadn't realised that although Holland is generally a flat country, their warehouse was at the top of a hill. They had opened the back doors of the container only to see the tennis balls go bouncing and rolling down the hill! That year we sent them 3 container loads and managed to finance 2 more sports shops with the profits.*

*Whilst at Hargreaves I was invited to join Round Table where I learnt so much in terms of accountability - doing what you say you are going to do - and if you are going to do a job, do it properly or don't do it at all. Those things stayed with me for the rest of my life. Round Table was very important to me and I met many people around the world who have remained tremendous friends. At Round*

## My friends and family

Table we did many things and in 1986 I became President. It opened all sorts of doors and avenues for me, the most memorable being the chance to row the channel in order to raise funds for charity.

When you are 40 years of age, you get 'thrown out' of Round Table which is probably the best rule so you get like minded people together. When we left, a group of guys often humorously called the Portsmouth 'Mafia' formed an ex-table group of 20 people called the Polo club because we played bicycle polo at our first meeting, completely wrecking the bicycles! We have kept going for 25 years and are all still great friends. I am the Chairman, or Head Lad, as they call it to this day.

During this period I became very interested in team building and in fact became more and more involved in team building over the years.
In 1988 when GB hockey won their gold medal at Seoul I arrived back from a trip and was asked to jump on a coach taking Havant 1$^{st}$ XI to a cup match in Coventry. The captain, David, told me that we had to have a manager for this particular semi-final and that I was 'it'. Thus started an amazing period. I managed the Havant first eleven in our first season in the newly established National League. We were runners up that year, National champions and cup winners the next 2 years, as well as the team playing in Europe. One thing I have always tried to do is to get out at the top, so after 4 years I passed on the mantel to Chris Picket at Havant, a great friend who took the club onto even greater heights including becoming European Champions. Throughout this era we were the 'Manchester

United' of hockey but along came England and I was asked to manage the men's team and to name my terms. The problem was it had been an in-house position before but I didn't want to leave Hargreaves so I took the job on a part time basis. It eventually became full time so I left Hargreaves to take up the role of team manager for England and Great Britain Men's Hockey Teams.

I went to three Olympic Games, Atlanta in 1996, Sydney in 2000 and Athens in 2004. I then trained the team managers from all 26 Olympic Sports for the British Olympic Association and had a peripheral role with the 2012 Olympics in London. I managed England and GB Hockey for 12 years with a lot of enjoyment and happiness but sometimes heartache. I consider myself very lucky to have been the longest serving manager in international hockey.

One of the most difficult situations that I have ever had to deal with was when one of the Havant team who was an Olympic gold medallist attended a training camp where doping controls were present and he was tested and found to be positive for social drugs, not performance enhancing drugs. He was subsequently banned. Because of the time that we had been together, the fact that he had lost his father at an early age and he was a customer at Hargreaves, my relationship with him was very strong. It broke my heart that this happened. He really was like a son to me and I felt that I had failed him.

Another incident occurred, in Malaysia in 2002 with the England team. In the very last minute of a match, our captain received a blow from a Pakistani stick which *severely damaged his throat. I had gone off to the press conference so did not know it had happened. When I returned, the physio advised me that the player had been taken to hospital. I followed with my liaison officer to where we thought he had been admitted but due to an administrative error on the part of the organisers we had been given incorrect information and he was not there. I telephoned contacts in Malaysia which led me to the ex-King who advised me to arrange for him to go to the University hospital where he would get someone to deal with my captain. Our arrival coincided with many Malaysians who had been involved in a gang fight. The ward and corridors were carnage with dead bodies all around in view of my player. One particular person in our vision was dead, the result of a baseball bat having been used on his head. I pointed out that in a civilised country the body would be covered up - which they duly did. Our captain was then transferred to intensive care where he had a tracheotomy and was stabilised. I fell out with our team doctor because he thought that after our player had stabilised his bed should be given to a Malaysian patient, but my duty of care was to my player.*

*This guy was due to get married two weeks later and I had to deal with a somewhat frantic fiancé and father who wanted to fly out immediately. We were trying to 'Medivac' him home. He couldn't speak and had to write everything down. I suggested to him that he was going to struggle to even get to his wedding in two weeks time, let alone be able to say 'I do'. He wrote a message on a piece of paper, which I still have to this day, which said 'When it happens it has got to be right. Please phone my fiancé and tell her'.*

*I was certainly not looking forward to it but after I had repeated what had been written on this piece of paper, she accepted it.*

*We 'Medivaced' him home having to go from Kuala Lampur, to Singapore, then to Hong Kong i.e. the opposite direction, in order to pick up a BA flight which was carrying sufficient oxygen for the entire trip back to London. Later, I visited him in a London hospital and saw him and his fiancé there. He has since made a full recovery and was appointed coach to the USA women's hockey team. They never got married and went their separate ways.*

*Whenever you play in hot climates the amount of water you need for players to drink is colossal. I have always had a degree of commercial awareness and upon arriving in one country with my liaison officer we went to a water manufacturing company and ordered a lorry load of water - thousands of bottles - which were delivered to our hotel and stacked around the walls in the doctor's bedroom. Other teams heard of this. I was fortunate enough to be able to sell them some of our water which resulted in me getting another half lorry load and making a profit on the whole trip for the team!*

*Unfortunately I have been involved in two bombings, one in Atlanta in Centennial Park when at 4 am I was woken up by the British chef de mission. He asked me to do a head count of my players as there had been a bombing in which one person had died. I did so and fortunately they were all present. However, one team manager in my block of flats in the Olympic village, representing table tennis, refused to get out of bed saying that his athlete was competing the next day and of course he would be in. That was my first encounter with 'jobs for the boys' where the president of a sports association had 'the perk' of going to an Olympic games as 'team manager' but without the ability or correct attitude. Since then the British Olympic Association has improved the recruitment of all team support staff.*

*The second bombing was in the Olympic qualifying tournament in Madrid in 2004. I was telephoned at 7 am asking if I had the tv Sky news on, which was reporting the Madrid bombings. I had to act quickly as we were playing at 10 am against the Belgian team, the winner advancing to qualify for the Olympic games which was effectively the culmination of 4 years work. No amount of telephoning around gave me any more information.*

*I called a team meeting, told all players and staff – 26 – that after this team meeting they were to go back to their rooms, telephone someone nearest and dearest in the UK, advise them that they were safe and that they would be incommunicado until approximately 1 pm, when they would phone them again. They should then turn off the telephone, turn off the television, get in the right mind set for what might happen but to focus on the game ahead for which they had worked for four years. I then told them to report to the lobby, as directed, with kit. Nothing changes, we go there to win. Transport arrived on time but upon reaching the stadium many people were in tears as some of their work colleagues had been killed. We started the game on time. We were told that 7 people had been pronounced dead. By the time the game was over the figure was 77 dead.*

*The organisers offered to abandon the tournament but the Spanish government refused to bow to terrorism. All the teams agreed to stay on except the Canadians. However, I insisted that our security was upgraded on all transport and that we put a curfew on the players within the hotel – we still had two matches to play. The biggest problem that we had was the lack of any communication either through the Foreign Office, or locally, and therefore we had to make up our own mind as to how we could deliver the duty of care for the players. The players' main concern was for their families who had come to watch them so we arranged for families to come into our hotel for safety. As the day and evening went by it became evident that the worst was over and the following day we tried to get back to normal.*

*It was a salutary lesson on crisis management. When I returned to England, the England football team manager, Sven Goren Erikson, invited me to Soho Square to the Head Office of the Football Association so they could learn what we had done as they were about to embark on a trip to Portugal for the European Cup. It's not rocket science, just common sense, making sure that the people for whom you are responsible are the top of the agenda.*

*In 1998 I was asked by Portsmouth City Council to try to help Portsmouth Football Club which had gone into administration. Quite quickly, we managed to raise £250,000 both from formal donations from companies and individuals and from tins being shaken throughout the city. There was a good deal of aggravation with acid being thrown on people's cars and strange people standing outside my house. Despite this we were very proud of our achievements. The City Council gave us an office and helped with our overheads when we were fundraising. When Milan Manderic took over the club I offered him the money that we had raised. He asked what I wanted in return for the money and I said for someone to sit on the board. He refused the request and refused to accept the money. He said we should give it back which we endeavoured to do.*

*On a personal note, I married my first wife when I was 26 and had one son. He has 4 children by 2 different wives – must run in the family! I was married to Monica for 6 years. I was travelling all over the country playing sport and my wife obviously saw my love of sport as a lack of love for her which is probably why she had an affair. I now understand and accept that.*

*I then had an affair with an airline hostess who was my first wife's best friend. If I'm truthful I thought if you are doing that so I am I. I eventually married her and had 2 sons. My second marriage was for 24 years. She was a brilliant mother but we grew apart. I was finding all sorts of reasons and excuses for going away for various reasons and I started to look elsewhere! That was quite a difficult period in my life. I don't feel entirely comfortable with the way I dealt with it, but we remain friends. Actually, I can say that about both my ex wives. I have managed to keep a reasonable relationship with them and would always help them out in times of crisis if it were necessary.*

*I then lived with someone for 5 years. We didn't get married but ran a business together. She told me one day that she didn't want me to live with her anymore. So I moved out. It was just before Christmas 2008. In the October I had been to a dinner for Havant Hockey Club players who were going to Argentina on tour. I had a very enjoyable evening sitting between two very pleasant ladies one of whom was June whom I married.*

*I decided I wasn't going to spend Christmas by myself so I made a list of eligible ladies whom I might ask to accompany me to functions. I first thought of June who I had known as an acquaintance since she was 17 and asked her if she would accompany me to a formal dinner. It was a very nervous phone call from my point of view, I know not why. She accepted and then I thought I had better get to know her a bit more beforehand so I invited her out. Obviously trying to impress, I took her to a Michelin star restaurant in Petersfield where she immediately complained about the napkin being damp and the fact that they were rushing us. I thought "What have I got here." On another occasion, I asked her to come to the house where I was staying so that I could cook a meal for her. An enjoyable evening ensued and she went home at about 11 pm much to my disappointment! The next morning a knock on the door alerted me to June standing on the doorstep with a paper bag. She walked past and said, "I just thought you might need this," going upstairs to the lavatory where she liberally spread bleach around the toilet bowl. She then left and went on to work. I was left open mouthed. Such were the first few encounters of what is a wonderful relationship.*

## My friends and family

*During the Christmas period I went on a singles holiday that I had booked before I became involved with June. I wished I hadn't booked it. All sorts of goings on between the guests ensued but I was so in awe of my new found love that I was as good as gold and spent most of my money on telephone calls back to England to June. She is so pragmatic.*

*Whilst at her house one evening we had just had supper with friends. I opened my mail which I hadn't had time to read. One letter was from my landlord/friend who said that they needed the house back by 1st March – it was now the end of January. "You can stay here if you like, you might as well, you spend most of your time here anyway," was June's response to the letter. I was gobsmacked but gladly accepted. We bought a house together in August that year and then got married the following May. As I said at the beginning, I have never been so happy in my life.*

----ooOoo----

Do you know, I'm still smiling? I just went to the funeral of David's father, John, who was 92 when he died. All the women in David's life turned up and sat in the front row at the crematorium. I wish I had taken my camera. I bet they were 'spitting blood' when they heard David say, what a wonderful wife June was and how well she had supported him!

I can't imagine having had that many serious relationships not to mention casual flings! Goodness me, I don't know how David got away with it and then to land up with June. I find it hard to comprehend.

Doreen, another pal of mine from the War was just the opposite of David. Doreen's first boyfriend was killed during the War and she is still married to her second boyfriend. I met her recently whilst I was queuing in the bank. She was looking really glum. She'd just been to the funeral of her best pal, Bunty. She had been asked, by Bunty's husband, to write her memories of their friendship. It's not surprising but many of my friends' memories are about the War. Anyway, I asked if I could have a copy of what she had written as I remember Bunty well......

*It was 1944 and I was sitting with a number of other wrens awaiting orders as to where we were going to be drafted on our next posting. We were in a rather large high-ceilinged room in one of the many Victorian blocks in the Royal Naval Barracks, Portsmouth. It was a bleak November day, the room was freezing cold. The wren sitting next to me evidently had a bad cold – she was shivering violently. She was a very attractive girl, with dark, wavy hair, and beautiful brown eyes, which a friend of mine was later to remark, "would fetch a duck off a pond".*

*A female officer had taken our details - the usual, name, rank, number and previous establishment, and then gone off, presumably to arrange transport etc. but our guess was she was tucking into a nice hot lunch. I exchanged names, hometown, and various naval experiences with my shivering neighbour, for whom I was beginning to feel very sorry.*

*The fire was made up in the grate, but when I suggested we light it, the general feeling was that we dare not break the rule that 'no fires are to be lit until after 5.00pm'. "Well, I'm going to light it;" I announced, "my friend here is not well, and if anything is said we all take the blame, OK?" It wasn't with quite a few of them, but I lit it anyway, and before long my friend was feeling much better – she was almost sitting on the fire! About an hour later the officer returned, carrying several files. She put them on the table, opened one, glanced at it, then looked up and asked,*

*"Who lit that fire?" Near silence, but several glances came my way.*
*"All right," she said, "if no one is going to own up, a report will be sent to the CO (commanding officer) of your new establishment, and you will all be punished in due course."*

*I could feel that I was going to be most unpopular in my new establishment so decided to own up. "I'm sorry, ma'am, but my friend Hughes has a very bad cold and was shivering so I lit the fire."*

*"And you are?" she demanded in a steely voice,*

*"44746 Bowdler, D, ma'am"*

*"A report will go with your draft, Bowdler, and your new CO will punish you accordingly." She smirked.*

*My new friend was most upset and wanted to take the blame instead, but I told her not to worry. We now knew we were both going to the same ship, – this is a naval term which may mean a ship or any other naval establishment - so I insisted she shared the spud-bashing, or confinement to quarters or whatever punishment I was given. As it happened we never heard another word about it and could only assume the CO thought it too trivial to warrant his attention.*

*Later that day a Navy truck took us to HMS Dryad in the village of Southwick and after an introductory tour of the establishment we were taken to our quarters, Soberton House, about five miles away. This was a large country house built around a quadrangle, which the Ministry of Defence (MOD) had taken over for the War. Most of the wrens were allotted a large cabin in the front of the house.*

*I moved quickly to get a double bunk near the window for my new friend, Hughes, and me. We chatted and sorted out our kit. She re-read a letter from her mother, which she had only had time to glance at when she picked it up earlier that morning. It began with 'My dear Bunty' and she explained it was her mother's pet name for her as she had been such a bouncing baby. I called her Bunty, teasingly after that, but as there was another Dorothy in our crowd, the name caught on, and she was Bunty Hughes to everyone.*

*I admired her courage that night as she knelt beside the bunk to say her prayers. If anyone had sniggered I am sure I would have hit them. As she wasn't feeling well, I let her have the top bunk (always the favourite) without the usual toss of the coin, which was going on elsewhere in the cabin. However, when the alarm bell went off at 6.00am Bunty forgot where she was and fell off – straight through the soft top of her suitcase. Fortunately, I had a sail-makers palm and needle and some waxed twine so was able to repair it by the time she went on leave, but she never slept on a top bunk again.*

*How cold it was that winter, and Soberton Towers was like a barn. The galley was officially out of bounds, but we would sneak down there at night and while one stood guard, the other made cocoa on the big Aga cooker. I heard from my mother that they had killed a pig at home and she was sending me some faggots. They duly arrived but the problem was how to heat them and then eat them. We were not allowed to have food in the cabin. However, nothing ventured, nothing gained. I posted my friend Hughes at the top of the stairs - the danger signal was a loud fit of coughing - whilst I dashed down to the galley and put the faggots in the oven. Then back to the cabin to wait for half an hour while they heated up.*

*I explained to the interested others how they were made. Faggots had never been part of their diet, I am afraid, the same as caviar had never been included in mine. Time was up. I took my seaman's jersey to wrap around the dish as much to disguise it as to keep it hot. Before we reached the stairs to the galley a strong smell of onions wafted along the corridor. Panic stations! We got those faggots back to the cabin at a rate of knots, then when we were halfway through eating them the lights went out.*

*Someone had a torch, and went to see what had happened. It turned out that Manuela Sykes, who was the helpless type, had gone to the attic to do some ironing and put the plug in the wrong socket thus fusing the lights.*

*Falling over the ironing board and bumping her head was no more than she deserved for bringing a load of officers down on us. One came to our cabin to see if we were all right then asked what that funny smell was. I told her the window was open and it was coming from outside. Actually it was coming from under the bedclothes where I had put what was left of the faggots. When she had gone Bunty and I dissolved in fits of laughter, which soon stopped when we discovered she was sitting on the faggots.*

*Manuela was a very intense person. I seem to remember her mother was an author and an authority on some intellectual subject or other. Be that as it may, it happened that the son of some Dutch friends of hers came with the crew of his ship to HMS Dryad for training. As instructed by her mother, Manuela contacted him and they went out and about together when off duty. She fell in love with him. This was her first love affair and she was totally smitten. Bunty, being a good listener, got a detailed account of the effect this was having on her life.*

*At bedtime, sitting on her bunk rolling up her hair in paper, Manuela would pour out her feelings. No one had ever loved as she did! Then one night returning to quarters from a date, I was met by a distraught 'agony aunt' Hughes. "Dot, you have got to come with me to search the ground for Manuela. The Dutchman has told her he is more or less engaged to a girl in Holland, and she is almost suicidal." More girls turned up armed with torches, and we set off in different directions. It was a horrible night, wet and foggy. I thought Sykes could have been a bit more considerate and waited for a frosty moonlit night as a branch knocked my hat off and bushes snagged precious stockings!*

*Eventually we reached the lake, and after discussing its awful possibilities we decided to backtrack to the house and report to the duty officer, who could then organise a proper search party. This done, we went back to the cabin to dry off and await the outcome of events. I certainly did not expect to find Manuela sitting on her bunk rolling up her hair. Apparently she had shut herself up in the attic to come to terms with the most traumatic experience of her life.*
*Sometimes we did not take the truck back to quarters, but caught the local bus to Wickham. On the corner of the Square, there was a sweet shop-cum-café where we enjoyed a lovely pot of tea and oodles of bread and dripping. The tea cost two pence, the dripping, sixpence. The only drawback was we had to hitch a lift back to Soberton as there was no evening bus service.*

*On the whole, we enjoyed our work at Dryad. In fact, it could be great fun making up mock battles on the master plot in the control room, used to train the ship's crews, who worked on the plots in the replica of a destroyer and aircraft carrier. Many of the wren plotters were from high society in civilian life. In our section there were a couple of 'Ladies', several 'Honourables', and many with double-barrelled names, but service life is a great leveller and we really did get on well for such a mixed bunch.*

*It was very rural in Soberton. At night, owls hooted from the old church tower and two great Danes, left behind by the owner, padded around the corridors of the house at all hours. It was difficult to get transport to and from either Portsmouth or Fareham so we were delighted when, after a few months, new quarters were found for us in the Solent Hotel on Southsea seafront. This meant we could go to the cinemas, shows on the pier and to the theatre.*

*Bunty was lucky and had 14 days leave over the Christmas holiday. I remember how lonely and fed up I was listening to Handel's Messiah on Christmas Day, all alone in the recreation room. The day she was due back had been one of those when everything seemed to go wrong. I was glad to take an early evening bath (in the regulation five inches of water) then relax in my new snazzy red and black pyjamas, and thick seaman's jersey and socks. Our unheated cabin was an attic room with four double bunks and we all dressed up to go to bed.*

*About 8.30 pm someone yelled up, "Bowdler, your friend Hughes is on the phone." Fearing she was ill or something and not coming back I dashed downstairs.*

*"Oh, I am glad you are there, could you come and help me? I've found a young boy wandering round the street looking for his mother. She left him in the house with his two little*

sisters and one of them is feeling ill and keeps crying. I think she has a temperature - I don't like to leave them. Could you come and look for the mother? I think she is in a pub somewhere."

"But Bunty, I am in my pyjamas," I wailed.

"Put your bell-bottoms on top of them and hurry." She then gave me the name of a side street near the Guildhall and said she would get the boy to look out for me - then her money for the telephone ran out. In a pub? I thought. Doesn't she know there is one on every corner of every street in Portsmouth? Nevertheless I did as I was bid and went as fast as I could. There was no hope of getting a bus along the Parade, up to the terraces and round by the Duke of York pub. No point going in there until I had a name and description, then I saw the boy, or rather, he saw my uniform and shouted.

There was Bunty on the sofa nursing a child with another sitting beside her. A miserable fire was smouldering in the grate. In fact the whole scene was miserable. "Could you try and find something to make a cup of tea before you go to look for the mother – I can't put this child down." Bunty could never go for long without a cup of tea.

I eventually found the mother. It was a familiar story in those wartime days; her husband was in the army. She had to have a bit of fun, didn't she - the kids were all right when she left. I didn't say a word. My friend, Hughes, said it all.

*We were very quiet as we walked back to the Solent Hotel, taking it in turns to carry her suitcase, which weighed a ton. Then she spotted my red and black pyjamas hanging down below my bell-bottoms and out came the laughter, which was never very far from the surface!*

*At last we were given our own quarters, Redlands, a small block of four flats overlooking the canoe lake in Southsea. Ours was a lovely front room with a bay window on the first floor. In it were four double bunks, and once again we managed to get one almost in the window. A chest of drawers was allocated to every two persons, which gave us two long and one short drawer each. The top of the chest was usually covered with personal knick-knacks, books etc which the other inmates respected.*

*The night we moved in was a bit chaotic, so I suppose Pam McMillan could have been excused for picking up Bunty's bible, but not for reading out loud, the dedication inside the cover. It had been given to her at the orphanage where she spent some unhappy years as a child. "Oh, how quaint," said McMillan in her affected voice. "I've never met anyone from an orphanage before, was it fun?" Utter silence. Having been a foster child myself, I could feel the fury rising in me, but Bunty with great dignity said, "May I have my bible, please? If you haven't got one, Pam, you are welcome to borrow it at any time."*

*The D-Day landings were planned from Southwark where we were stationed. The tension was tremendous for everyone who had put so much effort into the whole thing, but nothing like it was for the boys who had manned the landing craft. When they came back after D-Day, they had left as young, carefree boys and come back as old men. The experience of seeing people shot, killed or blown up had affected them badly. When the boats came back, that was horrible too; we had to clean up the landing crafts from the effects of the battle. It was August. It was hot, it was horrid. There were only us girls doing the cleaning. One girl was sick and refused to go back and do any more.*

*At last it was VE Day. The captain addressed the whole ship's company of HMS Dryad from the balcony above the portico of Southwick House, which is of course where Monty and Eisenhower planned and carried out the D-Day operation. We sang the national anthem, and then it was 'caps' off and 'three cheers' for the King. The rest of the day was ours, he said, but the chaplain was conducting a communion service in the village church for those who wished to attend. Bunty and I decided to go and so did Rogers. Although it was such a wonderful day, it was also very sad. It was good to know no more lives would be lost, at least not in Germany. The war in the Far East was still going on, but it was impossible to forget all the fear and heartache of the previous six years.*
*My boyfriend had been a Mosquito pilot. He was killed as he tried to land his damaged plane after a pathfinder mission. Many more old school friends had gone too, and boys I had known in Combined Operations perished on D-day. I thought of them all and I am sure the other girls had similar thoughts as we travelled back to Southsea.*

*A very noisy Southsea it was - every ship's siren and air raid siren was going, car horns were blazing, people were singing. It was bedlam! For lunch that day there was a piece of spam, dehydrated potatoes and a few carrots followed by a plum duff and watery custard. Several girls decided to go to London, if they could get on a train, as that was where everyone wanted to be. The First Officer came into the dining room and said that wrens in quarters had been asked to act as hostesses to foreign ships' companies in port. Four Norwegian crews had been assigned to us.*

*With our two strapping Norsemen, who didn't speak a word of English, Bunty and I made our way to the Guildhall, where it seemed hundreds of people were milling around singing and dancing. Not surprisingly, we became separated in the melee. My escort and I made our way to the Guildhall steps, which I thought would be a good vantage point to look for Bunty. Some marines were trying to climb on top of the stone lions. I pointed them out to my companion, who thought I was indicating that I wanted to get up there too. He grabbed me, lifted me up on to his shoulders and started climbing. Frantically I made him put me down again, but in the crush we fell, knocking over several other people. Luckily Bunty happened to notice the commotion on the steps and pushed her way through the crowd to come to my rescue. I am not at all clear how we eventually formed into some sort of parade, but with various bands leading us we finally reached the Savoy, having travelled most of the way on the shoulders of our Vikings. I think they were afraid we might be trampled underfoot.*

*Somehow or other, we ended up inside the Savoy and were on the balcony surrounding the dance floor when the King's speech was broadcast, but we didn't hear a word of it - the noise was too great! At night, there was dancing on the pier but when we got there it was full and there were no more admissions. This did not daunt our friends, however, they merely lifted us up and over the turnstile, then vaulted over themselves. We had hardly got inside when some crazy Yank caught hold of me and swung me round in the jitterbug. In one particularly acrobatic movement he let go of my hand too soon and I landed beside the drummer on the bandstand. That was enough! I could see Bunty was having her problems too and as soon as I could get hold of her, we decided to call it a day and make our way back to barracks and bed.*

*It was sometime later, though, that we got into our bunks. The cabin was full of exhausted wrens, swapping experiences. In between peals of laughter, Bunty explained the reason for my dishevelled appearance. Suddenly there was a loud knocking coming from the window. Someone opened the curtains (no more blackouts) and there peering in, were our Norwegians. They had come to say goodbye, via the ropes, which went from the window to the ground as a sort of fire escape. Practically the whole crew were out there and we decided there was nothing for it but to get the duty officer's permission to take them in the galley and make them some cocoa, then hope they would make their way back to the ship. They did after giving us their home addresses, making us understand how welcome we would be there when things were back to normal.*

*Life was much more relaxed after VE Day. It was as though we had come through a long, dark tunnel into the light. People were happier and seemed to laugh and smile* more easily. Little girls love to tell you about their bosom friend. Bunty was my bosom friend. She was loving and loyal with a gift for laughter and a sense of the ridiculous. I loved her.

----ooOoo----

Some people appear to find it very hard to make real friendships - it's as though they don't know how to make friends. I guess that also applies to relationships. I wonder if that is why we have so many broken marriages nowadays? Children spend so much time on computers it seems to me that they miss out on a lot of human contact. I go to all sorts of clubs and societies. There is always someone with whom to chat; have a laugh or even a cry. The young people today hug each other a lot more than we ever did or even do but it seems to me rather superficial. Lots of them say 'love you' when I am sure they don't mean it or even know what they are talking about. Seems a crazy habit to me!

Talking about love reminds me of someone I knew years ago called Terry. She had several disastrous relationships and then, aged 69, she met a guy also called Terry. They have so much in common it is great to see. Terry has had such a interesting life:

*I was born in Whitton near Richmond in 1941. I always did ballet as a young child and other dancing. I wanted to be a ballerina and at the age of 11 I went to the Royal School of Ballet. They measured me and told me that by the age of 17 I would be 5 feet 7½ inches tall and they only took students up to 5 feet 5 inches. I was very disappointed as I had set my heart on it. So at the age of 11 I went to the Corona Academy which was a performing arts school.*

*My sister was ice skating at the time so I decided to try it – ballet on ice. I loved it! I had taken my exams by the age of 17 and I started teaching skating at Streatham ice rink. I skated and taught skating until I was 24, then I was head hunted for 'Holiday on Ice' by an American company to teach the new artists coming into the show and to skate myself in the show.*

*I toured the whole of Europe and Scandinavia with the show, non-stop for 2½ years. 'Holiday on Ice' was really hard work. I would be on the ice at 10 am teaching and training, and then we would be doing 2 shows a day. In Paris we did 3 shows a day so your whole life was skating. We never saw the cities we played in because we would finish the show at say 11pm, drive through the night and open the next day at somewhere say 500km away. We would literally kip down for a couple of hours, have some black coffee and chocolate to keep awake, and then perform the next day.*

*Helsinki, Stockholm, Gothenburg, Copenhagen, Dortmund, Essen, Cologne, Stuttgart, Paris, Nante, Rheims, Nice, Bologna, Rome, Florence, Turin, Genoa, Grenoble – you name it we skated there. Athens was wonderful! We played in the old Olympic stadium there. They had to put a bubble over the ice to stop it thawing. We would skate at 9 pm at night and our showers were a pull string and bucket. The toilet was a hole in the floor – that was the* worst, but generally the conditions were OK wherever we went. We travelled from A – B all the time. Going to Helsinki, we were on an icebreaker to get us there. We had 2 nights on the boat which was great. We were full on the whole time. In Warsaw we were doing 2 shows a day but as the shows were so successful we had to do 3 shows a day. The only days we got off were Mondays in Paris as there were no shows.

The show always had a story. It was not just an ice review – we did Cinderella, Zhivago, Gypsy. It was a wonderful ice show with a very high standard of skating.

I had a fabulous time. There were 100 in the company. We had our own orchestra and conductor, we had our own engineers. It wasn't always an ice rink where we skated but may be a sports arena. The engineers went ahead. They laid the pipes and sand and sprayed it with water which made the ice. They then went back to the previous show after we left to clear up.

When we went from town to town there were quite a few of us who had caravans. The conductor was in charge of finding our campsites so we drove in convoy. We plugged in our electricity and that was that. The caravan was my home.

I had a bad fall on the ice where I fell on my coccyx and lost the use of my legs – paralysed. I was in Milan when this happened and a very good urologist gave me a lumber puncture. Slowly the use of my legs came back. I stayed in hospital in Milan for 3 weeks. After the fall my skating was never quite the same. I left the show and came back to England. I did a 6 week TV series in 'Carnival on Ice' and I also did a couple of Wembley shows.

I was very lucky to be a skater. It is a wonderful, wonderful sport and to have it as one's job is a bonus. I am still in touch with many people from the show - in fact someone from Australia has just been to stay. I taught her and her identical twin sister to skate back in the late 50's. They continued to skate with 'Holiday on Ice' for some time after I left.

Lots of us still keep in touch. Three years ago we had a big reunion in Nice. Four days of cocktail parties, a ball and the new ice show opening in Nice which we attended. We had the most incredible cocktails on the beach and we also made the Guinness Book of Records on the Promenade des Anglais. It was the longest chorus line in the world. A helicopter came along and filmed us doing a kick line holding shoulders wearing 'Holiday on Ice' yellow tee shirts. 'Holiday on Ice' has been going for about 60 years.

Life was such fun but very tiring. I think I fell because I was tired. It was really a wonderful part of my life, being able to skate every day and enjoy the company of 100 people.

I retired at 31 and have not skated since.

At 31 I was having a rest when a girlfriend rang and said, "We need someone to help in the design department of Medfern Interiors." I went there as temp and left 3½ years later having been groomed through all the departments of interiors, learning the trade. I was then headhunted to go to work for a company in Boreham Wood in Hertfordshire as a director of an interior design business. I worked there for 2 years and the gentleman who owned the company was elderly and wanted to retire. I decided then to open my own company in the late 80's which was called Solomon Interiors in Notting Hill Gate, London doing commercial interiors which had been part of my training. All of my existing clients came with me. As well as an interior design company I opened a curtain factory in the unit next to mine. My design work was aimed at the '5-star hotel' market and private hospitals. I employed 15 people – 7 curtain makers plus designers and admin staff. I kept going until I was 60 in 2001.

I was first married when I was 19 for 4½ years but he was unfaithful. I was then married to Cyril for 9 years who retired to Spain but I didn't like Spain so the marriage broke up. I was then with my third husband for 26 years. He was born close to my home and I had known him all my life yet he was unfaithful. That finished in 2002. I then had a partner who had cancer who died in 2009 after we had been together for 5 years.

I was introduced to Terry in 2010. A girlfriend of mine met Terry on the plane coming back from South Africa. They were chatting and she said "I have a girlfriend who has also lost her partner to cancer and who has similar interests to you". She arranged for us to meet. My friend, her husband, Terry and I had lunch and that was the beginning of our relationship. We are incredibly happy and have an extremely fulfilled life. We were lucky to find each other. We were married in January 2014 in South Africa.

## My friends and family

*Needless to say, I have had a very full life!*

---ooOoo---

As young girls, my friends and I always wanted to be ice skaters. It seemed so glamorous. It doesn't sound nearly so attractive now knowing about all the hard work and travelling involved. I must say I still do love their costumes and always watch ice skating when it is on the TV.

Terry is so lucky to meet someone with whom she gets on so well. Do you know that sadly, women outlive men about 8/1 that's why there are so many tea parties and events full of older women – the men are no longer with us!

Relationships are hard to maintain at the best of times but when older people become a burden on the next generation things can be really hard. Take where to live for example. When I can't live on my own, where should I go – to live with my daughter? I think not; to live with one of my great grandchildren? I know I could give them some of the money from the sale of my house to help them onto the housing ladder but I am not sure me being in the same house as any of them would work both from their point of view or mine. They have a life to live after all. From my perspective I probably wouldn't approve of the way they lived their lives. It would be very hard not to interfere. We get on really well now but I don't think being thrust together would work either.

## Memories are made of this

A friend of Charles' contacted me not long ago. He hadn't realised that Charles had died as he had been abroad for years. I said I would go to visit him in his warden assisted lodgings. I had always been fond of him. Going there really made up my mind that I didn't want that sort of accommodation either. Do you know, when I pressed the button to be allowed into the building there were several ladies just the other side of the entrance. They asked me whom I wished to visit. They seemed to know everything there was about Charles' friend; the fact he had a motorised scooter and went to the pub for lunch every day; that his daughter had cancer; that his son hardly ever came to see him and so on. Nosey I would call it! Anyway, when I went in to see him he said that there was only two men in the whole place so, "The women almost fight over us," he said laughingly. He said one would make him sausage rolls so the next day he had cakes from another women and they were always asking him to their flat for tea or to play cards with them.

Oh dear, I always thought that this might be an option but now I am not so sure. I did think about selling my house and buying one of those flats where there is a warden on hand but you are totally independent unless you need help. Patsy, in her usual sensible way, says, "What is the point in moving there now, and then having to move to a care home or nursing home later?" I suppose the other option is, when I can't care for myself, to have carers in to look after me but I am not sure I would like that.

Decisions, decisions, decisions, nowadays it seems to get more difficult to make decisions than ever before. I am not sure whether it is an age thing or whether we have so many different options it is just plainly hard to decide.

When my father-in-law had to go into a nursing home after a spell in a psychiatric hospital I remember we had to clear his house so we could sell it and pay for his care. I think the law has changed a bit since then but that was really the most awful experience. It was obvious he wasn't going to be able to live at home again, in fact probably never go out again, so we had to get rid of absolutely everything. Oh it was dreadful. We even had to search the pockets of his clothes so we could give them to the charity shops; throw so much stuff out and then close the door on a house where we had had many happy times. We had to behave as though he was dead when he was still very much alive.

Old people's homes are fine for some people but at the moment they are definitely not for me. I know there are good and bad ones and what suits one person would not suit another but for the moment I am burying my head in the sand and not thinking too much about it. The decision about when and where an old person should go into a care home or nursing home is often one of the most difficult decisions an older person or their family has to make if they become unable to make the decisions themselves. We see so many examples of poor homes or poor treatments on the television that it is quite scary to think that one day such a decision will have to be made by me or for me.

## Memories are made of this

Isn't it funny how, as we get older, we reminisce so much more. We think what might have been or should have been; if that had happened, things might not be that way now; if we had not met that person or married that person who knows what our life would be. I wonder if those who are young today will be this way when they are older? Their lives are so different from ours, so immediate, so transitory, so 'come day go day'. Will they want to remember or actually be able to remember?

**Part 3**

**Still doing what they do best**

I remember when I was younger there were strict rules/guidance on retirement. Women retired at 60 and men at 65. That was it. I don't think you were expected to do much else after that. Nowadays, anything goes. Some people take early retirement in their 50's if they have a good pension offer; others carry on until retirement age which I think is 68 for everyone now; others give up their main job and take on lesser stress related jobs such as in retail – I know this widower who on retirement from being Managing Director of an electronics company, got a job on the till at his local supermarket. It was fantastic for him, he had something to do each day and a reason to get up; he meets people and originally saw the job as another life challenge. He's coming up to 80 now and only works 1 day a week. As he is so good at French, a French family come in to the store whenever he is working, to speak French to him during the transaction........and then there are others who just keep on working. Take Mary for instance.

Mary is one of my keep fit friends and has lived in the Portsmouth area all her life. She is really lively and vivacious and everyone seems to like her. It was really funny the other day. I was listening to Women's Time on the radio when, can you believe it, Mary was being interviewed. She's 76 now and really very well known as an artist. I quickly pressed the record button on my music centre, so here it is:

*Welcome Mary to Women's Time I believe you have painted nearly 1000 pictures and that you plan to reach 1000 paintings in the next couple of years? I wonder if you would tell our listeners how you got started?*

When my friend and I were young we always drew. We loved drawing. I was absolutely obsessed but I didn't take up painting seriously until I was 45 years of age.

My brother went overland to Australia with his wife. Eventually he became assistant art master at Geelong Grammar School. He spent a couple of years in this post and did a lot of painting. He was in the art world and thought, why don't I do this on my own, so he set up a studio at his home and carried on painting. All the time I was in constant contact with him, as we are very close. He managed to sell a few paintings and he came home to England occasionally and sold them to the Fareham gallery.

I didn't start painting until my sons came up to their teenage years. I kept thinking, why don't I have a go? I did. Initially I painted on pieces of cardboard boxes covered with white emulsion paint. At about this time my brother came home to live and he and I started working together, he didn't exactly teach me but he gave me something to paint and then criticised it. Neither of us had any formal training.

'Your place or mine' became our sort of slogan in the early days as my brother and I used to phone each other up to see where we were going to paint, his studio or mine. Sometimes we would go out and paint in a field.

*When did you realise that people might buy your paintings?*

For about a year after I started painting I gave my pictures away whilst I was learning. Then there was an art exhibition in Wickham and that's where I first sold a painting, to someone I didn't know, it was most thrilling. I wrote all over my studio wall in pencil 'I've sold a painting'. Then I gathered all my courage and went to the Fareham gallery with my pictures. They said they would hang them. I was over the moon. After that my paintings did start to sell and the Fareham guy filtered a lot of them to someone in Cornwall.

*Did you have ambitions to hang your paintings in London or even to have an exhibition?*

After a while, my brother and I decided that it was time we broke into a wider market and the two of us took our paintings to London. We trudged the streets. First of all we had no luck and then by chance we went into a gallery in Avé Maria Lane near St Paul's Cathedral. The gallery also had a publishing company. They liked our work and said they would like to put on an exhibition.

That was the start. Not only did we have our London exhibition – 30 paintings each - but a coach load of people came up from Wickham. I was so nervous because of my lack of self belief. I got through it though. We had a wonderful evening and then the publishing company started to publish our work and our names became known. We had several joint exhibitions.

## Memories are made of this

*How did you cope trying to paint so many pictures and also run a home and look after a family?*

John, my husband, adjusted to me being a full-time painter very well. When he was 55 he retired from his job and became house husband and also my business partner. He did the money side and I did the painting. John's role was pricing. We had no idea how to do it so we started charging so much a square inch. Gradually we grew into it and found what the market would pay. John chased payment of invoices too.

*Are you a disciplined person?*

I guess you would say I probably am. I worked every day from 10am to 3pm, 5 days a week. I usually get ideas for the next painting whilst working on the previous one. Lots of my friends wouldn't come round because they knew I was painting. For about 25 years I was working at that rate. I'm nearly on my thousandth picture now. I would still rather be in my studio than doing anything else.

I kept a 'bible' of all my pictures. I am now on 995. I will certainly do 1000 before I die. In my 'bible' I have kept a record of all my paintings, where they went and what happened to them, which exhibitions they went into, which ones were printed. It tells a story really and how the prices rose over the years.

My brother also gave me a good piece of advice – never get rid of anything you paint as you will be able to see how you progressed.

*Do you take commissions from other people for your paintings?*

I never do a painting that is specifically for someone. I once painted some dogs for someone. Also a woman asked me if I'd do two paintings as a surprise for her husband, which I did, but I hated it.

I like to paint what inspires me. I did still life for quite a few years then later I started to bring in a few leaves and flowers and it developed like that until about 1980. I suddenly thought if I am going to paint wild flowers then they ought to be where they grow naturally. I used to paint about 20 - 25 a year. I have always painted in oil.

*Apart from your first exhibition at St Paul's gallery, where else has your work been shown?*

Once we were published, then our work started to be seen in a much wider market. I've had exhibitions in America; I've been on American TV and had numerous exhibitions in this country. Some of my work has been printed onto mugs and plates and also made as a tapestry for people to sew. The tapestries, along with the silks, were sold by the National Trust. I met up with my old art teacher, Miss Gray, not so long ago, and she was very pleased to see what had happened to me.

*Would you like to tell our listeners about your family?*

My mother was a very beautiful woman who was born in the Forest of Dean. She was one of 9 children. She broke away from a very difficult family and moved to London on her own where she became secretary to a doctor. I'm told she was quite a 'flapper', a woman about town, a party goer, wore lovely clothes. I have since found out that she became pregnant by the doctor for whom she worked. He sacked her as she wouldn't get rid of the baby. She went to Portsmouth and had a baby girl but I don't know anymore of the story. Just think, I may have a step-sister somewhere. My mother then met my father. All his family lived in Portsmouth. I always had this idea that she hadn't been very well accepted by his family but now I know why.

My dad went off to War when I was 3. He was rescued from the Dunkirk beaches and he and my mother spent a short time together. My mother conceived my brother David during that time. Dad was then sent off to the Far East. He was captured by the Japanese and worked on the Burma railway. He had a really bad time. The men were beaten even if they were ill. Dad died in squalor in the concentration camp.

Mum didn't know about dad's death until 1946. He was missing all that time. She put an advertisement in the local paper to ask if anyone had known her husband in Malaya. She had a letter back from an officer who was in the same camp as dad. According to one of his closest pals his last few days were marked by a strange tranquillity; that death was going to be an end to this living hell. At about this time mum got a letter from the War Office telling her dad had died of cholera and dysentery. My dad wouldn't eat just anything, whereas some men ate monkeys, and mice. My dad had unknowingly eaten diseased rice. He drank water from the river Kwai.

When mum had the information about my dad she lay in bed and cried for 3 days. I wasn't really aware of what was going on. I got in bed with her. My auntie said, 'There's no need for you to cry like that,' but I did.

*Oh how terrible! So what happened next?*

Anyway, there was this young man – he weighed only 4 stone when he came back to England - who had been in the same camp as my dad. He came to our house to give us messages from my dad. We were living in Portchester and it was there that he turned up at the door.

He was 12 years younger than her but mum and him became friendly and eventually got married. He had been jilted whilst away. I think she was pregnant with my second brother at the time; then she had my sister Sue, so there were 5 of us. He was a wonderful person and we called him Dad. He treated us all the same.

*What sort of person was your mother?*

Mum was a very strong woman. I think she thought that as my father had lost his life for his country, the country should give something back to his children. Mum wrote endless letters to MPs and the War Office and got grants for all of us to go to very good schools. She also got involved in every aspect of our life such as making ball gowns, school uniform, vetting boyfriends, helping with homework, supporting us at sports days and taking us to the beach and on holidays.

There was a lot of joy in my life. My friend and I used to cycle to Hayling. Her parents owned a beach hut there and we would spend the day with her family. We always loved the sea and were always in it. We also sang in talent competitions. We once won a competition on South Parade pier – we sang the Mamma Doll song in harmony. We have remained firm friends the whole of my life. We meet regularly for lunch to this day.

*Did you get on well with your step-father and was he a big part of your life?*

We were very poor. Dad worked in an ironmongery shop but I was mixing with lots of rich girls at school. I can remember being quite mean to him. My friend wanted us to go to the pictures. He said no, we can't afford it. She put a note through our letterbox saying I must go. I shouted at him, saying you are not my father. He slapped me and sent me upstairs. Eventually my friend wrote another note saying she was sorry.

Mum and my dad ran the FEPOW (Far East Prisoner of War Club) so we had a lot of other ex prisoners drifting in and out of our house as well as FEPOW dances, FEPOW conferences. They worked very hard. There were piles of papers everywhere. They wanted to give something back. It was a good childhood; we were not into fashion but into adventure. My friend's life was very different to mine but it didn't make any difference. I would go to hers for tea on Tuesdays and have a big fry-up. On Thursdays she came to me and we had lettuce sandwiches. Dad had grown the lettuces. We never compared.

Mum and dad were great party people. When they had a party they moved all the furniture out; families came from miles around, and all slept the night on the floor. It was a good marriage but my mother never got over the great love she had for John, her first husband.

*You have told us about your family. Are you willing to tell us about yourself?*

I left school at 17 and trained as a shorthand typist and got a job at the Portsmouth Building Society. My friend and I were going out with two boys for several years. They were RAF entrants. She eventually married Colin. I was still going out with Ted when John came along to the building society to audit the books. I can see him to this day in the back room in his navy blue pin striped suit. After several abortive attempts he asked me out. He sent a friend to ask me out so I took no notice, then he followed a bus on his bike which he thought I was on. The next day he actually asked me if I would go to the pictures with him. I was going out with both boys for a few days but John swept up in his father's car to take me out. I thought he was very handsome, there was no contest! We went out together for 6 years though we were engaged for 2½ of those and then we got married in 1959.

From the building society I went to an estate agents and then to Cosham police station. I always did secretarial work. Not only did it open my eyes to the seedier side of life but it was very interesting. They were a lovely bunch of lads. They handcuffed us together at our wedding. They found out from my mother where we were going on honeymoon and sent us some little pink booties in a little plastic container which one of the waiters brought to us on a silver tray. I worked at the station until I was pregnant with my first child. I had all these crazes so the cops went out looking for my cravings for me.

*Is there anything else about yourself or your family you would like to share with our listeners?*

I was very jealous as a young married person. I didn't have a lot of self belief or self worth and I was very jealous of John. He is a very gregarious person. There were occasions when I was consumed with jealousy. Thankfully now it has left me but it lasted quite a few years. I was at home with the children and he was out there, going to office parties etc. My real father was very jealous so probably I got it from him.

My brother, David, also had problems in his life. He and his wife had always suspected that their son was gay. When his son finally told the family they were devastated. My brother took it very badly. His paintings became dark and broody and he painted many rain scenes. He felt there was a curse on our family. My step father had died in his thirties, then another of my brothers died and later his son, who was also gay and died of AIDS.

John is now free and available more and I feel a bit mean to be always painting - plus the pictures are not selling so much these days. I used to take 5 or 6 to a gallery and they would take 5 but not any more. I am also enjoying more freedom to be with John.

Painting never became a chore, but I still have to paint but at a much slower rate. At this stage in my life I am thinking I might try other styles, such as my family in old costumes. Funnily enough, I have just had a commission to paint the Flanders Poppy Fields.

I was terribly shy in my youth, I blushed a lot. I hated going into a room full of people. My confidence has only come in the last 25 years. I think painting helped my self belief.

It has been a very good life. We are entering the 4th dimension now, that tranquil time.

----ooOoo----

Mary is such a lively person even now. She still plays tennis and golf, goes to exercise classes and rides her bike to the sea front to go for a swim. She even has her own website to sell her paintings.
I guess you would say that Mary's paintings reflect her personality. They are bright and vibrant and nowadays are mainly of flowers and scenery. The one thing I have against them is that sometimes, for example, Mary puts, say flowers, in a place where they couldn't possibly have grown – I guess you call that artistic licence.

I've heard that Mary is having a bit of 'an old age crisis'. She has decided she doesn't want to paint for profit any more. She is thinking of getting rid of all the paintings she has round the house – probably about 50 of them – selling them off quite cheaply and starting afresh "Painting just for me, painting just what I want, when I want". It will be interesting to see just what her paintings look like in this new (older age) phase of her life.

I really enjoyed Mary's story so thought I would find out a bit more about the radio programme. Apparently they are running a whole series about women who are in their seventies and still working. They've had journalists Joan Bakewell and Katherine Whitehorn, and the politician Shirley Williams. Last week they had someone else on the show who I know well. She is still doing what she does best and is also a friend of mine, called Ann. We met years ago when I was working at Southampton and we did some research together. We come from very different backgrounds yet we really get on famously. She is into her mid-70's now and yet she is still doing research at Oxford University where she is a professor. Here is Ann's interview:

*First of all I must congratulate you on being awarded an OBE. I believe David Willetts, Minister of State for Universities and Science, may have had a hand in this award?*

Thank you very much. Yes, I did do a lot of work for David so I suspect it was him who put me forward. I was 72 when I went to Buckingham Palace.

*Have you always been an academic, Ann?*

No, I started late so I still find this work fascinating, I did all the cooking and flower arranging in my 20's and 30's!

My father was ill from the time I was 12, so we were quite pushed financially. My parents were keen to get me out to work so at 16 I trained to be a secretary at Reading Technical College. Then I went to London and lived with my cousins. I was a bad secretary although I was quite dashing in those days - but didn't think about it. I was a good talker! When I was about 18/19 I worked as a secretary in New York. The US was amazingly liberated whereas in the UK life was quite constrained. I remember thinking I wouldn't ever get enough money to buy a house in the UK. In the US I realised women could do things. I met up with someone in New York and then saved up enough money to go round the world on a P&O ship, the Arcadia, with a friend.

We set off across America and then joined the ship in San Francisco. We didn't realise we needed money to eat so tried to persuade the other people on the boat to give us their soup or pudding. There were 6 or 8 of us to a cabin down in the bowels. We went to LA, Hollywood, Hawaii, surfing in NZ and Australia. Then we went to Ceylon and Sri Lanka. In India my friend met up with a boyfriend and disappeared so I went back alone through Aden, the Suez Canal and Marseille and got back to the UK just before Christmas. I was travelling for about 2 months.

I didn't know where I belonged – everyone seemed to have the same problem in London. In those days marriage was your career. Life was rather flat when I came home. I went back to London to work as a secretary and then went to work for a publishing company so I applied to agencies to work as a copy writer.

*Did falling in love change the direction of your life?*

I guess so. I met a widower, Alistair. That was in September and we were married the following July. We had a fun time in London but I was permanently pregnant. I lost 6 babies in all though I did have 3 healthy girls. Mentally, I needed something more so I started to train as a social worker.

I then got pneumonia and landed up in hospital so Alistair decided we should move out of London as he didn't want to lose another life. We moved to Hillbarn, near Marlborough, where we lived for 30 years. It was hard at first but I was used to country life. I went to Bath to finish my training. My older children were in school by that time. Before Bath I worked two days a week for a doctor doing research on child abuse.

*Once you completed your training did you actually become a social worker?*

I got a job in Reading working in child guidance. I was there for about 10 years working on the front line as a social worker. This was the mid 80's. I was then asked to go to teach in a further education college - that was a nightmare. You had to fill your teaching hours. You had to prepare your lessons out of nothing. About that time I signed up at Southampton University to work towards an MPhil – I did it one day a week. I said to someone in authority at the University, "I reckon this could be a doctorate," and they said "Why not". On a social work course to get a doctorate you had to be doing something worthwhile. I worked with a group of children who had a problem in that they soiled their pants.

*Would you say that you are primarily a researcher?*

I was always doing something with research. I was more mature than most others around me. I wrote to Southampton University (Soton) and said what about giving me a job. They 'ummed and arred' and then gave me a job at £14.000 pa, a drop in salary. I was teaching social work. I could only afford to take a drop in salary as I had a husband who could keep me in 'the manner to which I was accustomed!' Soton had a system of merit awards so my pay soon got back up to a reasonable level.

Alistair was hugely supportive. He is quite conservative but quite radical. There was a lot of pressure all around with people saying "Oh it will ruin your children's lives." Boulby, an author on bringing up children, was a dreadful person with his theories. He gave me a terrible conscience but I needed to do my work for my own sanity.

I was driving to Soton for about 2 years but I was in touch with a cognitive therapist. I then became a locum at Oxford one day a week. In April 1994 the Barings

Foundation gave me the money for some research which we called the Dolphin project. Dolphin was the first research project to ask young people what they thought. It was very influential. It was also a very innovative project where we met young people in care and their carers. Quite a few publications came out of that work. I later became a trustee of the Baring Foundation.
I then heard about a job that had come up at Oxford University. I was very unsure at that time as I didn't have a first degree so I was very lucky to get the job. The University kept me waiting for 2 months before offering the job to me.

*You seem to have landed some fabulous jobs. How have you managed it so consistently?*

I guess I was rather cheeky sometimes. I always kept my ear to the ground so I knew what was going on. I didn't mind asking, after all people can only say 'No'. I always grabbed my chances.

*So what was it like working for one of the world's leading universities?*

When I first went to Oxford I was rather subdued, then I realised that if you kept your head down you could do anything you wanted, so I decided to call my self 'The Centre for Research and Development for Parenting and Children'. After a year I called myself the Director. I didn't ask anyone I just did it! Nobody said I couldn't, I didn't have any supervision. This gave me an international brand which has taken me everywhere. Then a few people came to work for me. When I got money for research I could pay people – I was 'mother goose' for lots of young researchers.

The centre gave me a vehicle for other things, I raised over £1m in total for use on research. The centre was fun and we used to have seminars every autumn term around 'wellbeing'. We invited people from London, the House of Lords, the Department of Health. They all came and then we managed to get two edited book volumes out of it. With the second one 'Emotional Wellbeing of Children', we mixed up practitioners and academics, which was very rare in those days.

*I believe you did quite a lot of travelling in your work?*

I travelled a lot, I like travel. I would think of a place in the world that I would like to visit and then I would find a conference to go to. I had research money. With my centre, I also got invited to post communist countries. I went to Latvia, Hungary, the Czech Republic and then I became part of a team. It was a 3 year research project in Perm in Russia which was a closed city where they used to keep atomic weapons. The people were all ex weapons inspectors. We made 3 or 4 trips to Russia and then they came here for 3/4 trips. The leader's wife ran travel agencies. She was Renee Kalashnikov – Kalashnikov rifle!

*How did your career pan out after that?*

Somebody said I should get into longitudal data. I obtained some funding and found a research project to look at what happened to children in care later in life. We used a very large sample of children who had been in care over the past 30 years and put them into groups - 2 parents, 1 parent, disadvantaged, in care - and in every measure children who had been in care came out worst. They were 4 or 5 times more likely to have problems. The report was called 'What happened when they grew up?'

What I also found out was that children who were read to by their fathers did better in all sorts of ways. I looked at fathers as a measure. Then the next project was on divorce and we found where parents had rows and then divorced it was very bad for the children.

Then I did another project for Joseph Rowntree - also about fathers and based on the 1988 data We had wonderful fun with the fathers project, we went to India, Tel Aviv, Iraq, and Bagdad – 'Oxford research says fathers are good for children'. We actually had a 'measure' so they liked this. It brought fathers out of the woodwork. If you want to make a difference you have got to get your message 'out there'. The problem was the mixed message – separation and divorce.

*How has your life progressed in Oxford since the early days?*

I have become a professor because of my work – ad hominine – a distinction which I keep for the rest of my life. It is my own. Very few people have been awarded this in my department. You have to apply to the University. The department would never have recommended me. I was 'a pain in the butt' to them. They were far too comfortable. I was suggesting you should run social work and do research. I have to recognise the department though, because it gave me a base but it is still not a happy place there. Oxford has changed now; the only people appointed are the top people. Most of the 'old school' are gradually retiring.

*Have you any new work on the go?*

I was cheeky; I applied to be on the Council for the ESRC (Economic & Social Research Council) and was appointed. Ian Diamond, ex Southampton, a lovely man, wanted to promote social work. I was then asked to do things because I was on the Council, even though I was retired. I was asked to be on the Oxford Research Council. I re-wrote the ethics policy for the ESRC.

Then there was the Centre for Research into Parenting. We had all the stuff on impact and we had set up a course. A lot of the stuff I had been doing about fathers was impact stuff. Then I was made chair of the Government's Evaluation Committee. The Civil Service don't like outsiders; they don't like change but I sort of moved things along. You can only do 6 years. It was a fascinating time. There was £200m and I was involved in deciding where the money went. I was also on the University committee deciding on strategy.

*Are you looking for something new for the future?*

I have been made an academician for the Academy of Social Science and am on the Council of that - promoting social sciences more widely. I have also made links with

Professor Ma who is doing a study in Shanghai. I have made 5 or 6 trips there but then I realised I was too old. You have to make links much earlier. One of my contacts at the Chinese Academy was Professor Zheng. She contributed a chapter (in my book) about her research showing that lone children in China only wanted to have one child even though they are now allowed to have two.

*So how do you feel now?*

I started late so I still find this work fascinating, Oxford is really exciting. You have a wonderful 'brand' but you have to be very careful. As long as you don't bring the University into disrepute you are fine. The strategy is to employ good people and give them their head. There is little need to tell them what to do.

I still have a base in the department which means I have an identity. I am often in the office 3 or 4 times a week. I have an ongoing project - a web site for social workers on troubled children - which I have to evaluate. I can't imagine not doing anything.

*And what of your family?*

Family wise, I was always very involved. I have 3 grown up children and 7 grandchildren. We have done lots of babysitting and we pay for most of the grandchildren's education so I have to keep working! The children have given me lots of happiness. However, Tess, my daughter, had problems, which were very tricky and eventually she got divorced. She was having a very hard time so we tried to help her to come home from Croatia where she and her children lived. Legally it was complicated. I had done all that research but it didn't help me to help my daughter - conflict resolution!

I had a major operation about a year ago and I thought I had cancer which made me reflect. I thought I would be dead in 3 months. It was not malignant luckily.

*So how would you sum up your life?*

Somehow through it all Alistair and I have remained happily married. It has worked well in that Alistair likes his space and I like gadding off to far off places. There is no magic in it but somehow we were just lucky plus, of course, patience, and hard work. I have no regrets; I married well to a man who stood by me through all the problems. I have done things I never thought I would do. But somehow I always still feel slightly inadequate because I never went to university and never obtained a first degree.

----ooOoo----

Mary and Ann are two very different people but actually they seem very similar. They are still working well into their 70's but are working on their second careers but neither started on this second career until they were in their forties. They are both very ambitious people who managed to achieve so much by ability and also by having the nerve to ask where others wouldn't. They had to learn as they went along; to not be afraid of making mistakes and generally, at times, to have 'the cheek of the devil'. They also both have supportive husbands. I have a feeling that these two will manage their old age in a similar way to their lives.

Thinking about these two people reminded me of when I was deciding whether or not to retire. I was 65 years old. There was a brilliant speaker, Mike Sage. If ever he was speaking at a conference or meeting I always tried to go to hear him. One day, I went to a small conference in London where he was speaking. He was so dreadful and quite forgetful that it made up my mind for me there and then – I was no longer going to accept invitations to speak publicly. I decided I would go out now as people remembered me and not as some silly old codger. Grow old gracefully I say!

**Part 4**

**That's Life!**

Hooray! I've actually seen a GP who listened to what I had to say and took it on board. He wasn't patronising, or so busy he sounded disinterested. I went to see him, not because I was ill in the normal sense of the word, but because I felt lethargic, and dull. Since the beginning of the year when I was told I had an irregular heart beat I have seen 3 doctors at our local surgery.

The first one I saw late in the day - at about 4.30pm. He seemed so old and tired. He looked as though he should have retired some time ago, not still be working late in the afternoon. When he took out his hearing aid to listen to my heart beat I nearly flipped and walked out. The second one had a 'you and me' mentality. He thought he was right, so nothing I said would change his views even though I had seen, on the internet, that there was an alternative to the drugs he had prescribed. The third doctor listened, thought about things, discussed them with me and together we made the decision to change one drug at a time to see how things went. I almost felt better straight away.

Sitting here now, I just wonder whether all these people who are sitting around in old people's homes, in hospital wards or in their own homes are really lifeless or are they 'drugged up to the eyeballs'. Are they existing, rather than living? As soon as you reach 70 you seem to be given drugs even if you don't need them. Doctors seem intent on preventing heart attacks or strokes but have forgotten that people should live their lives to the full - which they can't if they are drugged too much. I watched an amusing film the other evening about old people in a home and how, led on by a new resident, some of them decided to stop taking their pills. They certainly seemed more lively and alert although the people running the home were not amused.

During the D-day celebrations in 2014 there was a man on the TV who had 'escaped' from his nursing home and travelled to France for the D-day celebrations. Good on him I say!

It's odd how everything about you seems to change once you reach 70. Oh, that dreadful number! Things seem to start to 'fall off', go bad or won't work! I had never taken tablets in my life until I reached 70 and then suddenly I needed tablets for blood pressure. Later I was put on beta blockers and Warfarin. I really resisted the Warfarin, but the doctor insisted. He also said my cholesterol was too high and wanted me to take more tablets. I resisted that, but can't now eat what I want - I even have to drink decaffeinated tea. Other people I know have heart problems, back problems, eyesight troubles - goodness me I am not sure it was worth the wait! At least I don't have to wear incontinence pads like several of my older friends. Oh, I would hate that!

Also, by the time you are 70 most people have to get up in the night to go to the toilet. I know people who get up 4 or 5 times a night, and often can't get back to sleep afterwards. Certainly some tablets make this worse but so does what you eat or drink. It's all very well eating healthy salads or green vegetables but oh, they do make you pee rather more – white wine and fish are the worst offenders for me!! I know people who change their eating/drinking patterns so that they don't have to get up quite so often.

Recently I read that we should keep carrying our shopping bags because it is good exercise. Apparently even knitting is good for you as using a pattern keeps the brain active. We have also been told to keep walking up stairs and not get a lift fitted on the stairs.

Talking about stairs, I seem to spend all day going up and down stairs. I've got these fine framed specs and can never find them. I put them down on my desk upstairs and then go downstairs to do something, but I then need to go back upstairs before I can start because I need to find my specs! This sometimes happens 3 or 4 times a day so you could say I am getting exercise - but rather annoyingly!

A while ago I had an operation for a prolapsed vagina which turned out to be much more complicated than I had expected and in fact the operation lasted 5½ hours. After the operation I was given some tablets which were meant to help with the healing process. I have a history of being allergic to a wide variety of medicines yet the consultant and my GP didn't think that I might be allergic to this drug. In truth I didn't too, but when it became impossible for me to control my 'waterworks' I became desperate. One day, about 2 weeks after the operation, I became really despondent, thinking I was going to be this way for the rest of my life, when it suddenly occurred to me that it might be the, so-called, healing drug. I stopped taking it. Within 24 hours things vastly improved and within another 48 hours I was totally well. My friend Norman looked the drug up on the internet and do you know what it said? 'Possible allergic symptoms – urine incontinence'!

When I was in hospital there was one nurse who insisted that after an operation every patient had a pain killer each evening even if they said they didn't want it. I think she thought she would get a better night duty if her patients were drugged. She was so insistent I took the tablet from her and then threw it away.

Not long after I 'came to' after the operation the woman in the bed opposite said to me that I had just had a text come in. When I read it, it made me laugh although this wasn't a very good idea knowing the extent of the operation! My friend had written, 'How's your designer vagina now?'

Norman has had a slight problem with his heart. When he went to the hospital to see about it they gave him statins, beta blockers, blood pressure tablets and aspirin. He thought he would start taking them slowly so he took the blood pressure tablets and aspirin first. He felt fine and in fact the slight pains in his chest disappeared. However, his GP said he should take the other drugs so Norman started taking the beta blockers with disastrous effect. His personality changed. He felt lethargic, like a zombie and said if it means staying alive and feeling like that then I don't want to feel that way. He said he felt like the people in an old person's home. You are alive but it looks as though you are in storage, not living, so he stopped and changed back to his normal self. He has never got round to taking the statins. I know someone else who was given beta blockers and he said, "I have no energy, no interest in anything, no sex drive, no vitality. What's the point, just in case it stops me having a heart attack?"

And what about sleeping tablets? How many people wander about in a permanently dazed state because of the tablets they have taken to make themselves sleep? I don't know, but I bet, most of the inhabitants of any old people's home are given sleeping tablets. They can be addictive too so you get into a habit of not sleeping, taking the tablets, feeling sleepy during the day so not sleeping at night so taking more tablets.

I have often read that as you get older you need less sleep than before. I don't know about that as I seem to need 8 hours sleep every night. I wonder if it is because often older people don't do very much actively with their life so don't get tired or if their body is messed up because of the tablets they take? I know lots of older people who have several naps during the day. I wonder if that's what makes them not sleep at night?

'Power nap'. That's a new one on me. Apparently the latest recommendation is that it is good for athletes to rest up and have a short nap of say 20 minutes during training but the rest of us have been doing it for ages!

Hoorah! I'm so excited. I've finally got round to making a Living Will. I've been meaning to do it for ages and now it's done. It really was so simple. Norman downloaded the form; I filled it in on the screen; printed it off and signed it. 'Hey presto' it's done!

If, say, I have a car accident or a stroke or develop dementia, and to use the legal term, 'lack the capacity' to make or tell someone of my decision, doctors must act in my best interests. That is, except if I've made an advance decision, in other words, signed a 'living will'. This allows you to indicate that you wish to refuse certain types of medical treatment should you be unable to make or tell someone of a decision about your treatment in the future. A living will must be respected by the medical professionals who are providing your care, whether or not they think it's in your best interest.

I've just been watching a debate on the television about 'the right to die'. Someone was going to the High Court in London to try to get a ruling that, when their quality of life is so poor and there is no chance of improvement, the doctors or family should be allowed to let the person die without the fear of prosecution. I know some people go to Switzerland to allow this to happen, but I would want to die in my own country. Providing adequate safeguards are in place, I think we should be allowed to die peacefully. I know I joke with my family about 'giving me a pill' when I am no longer in a fit state to live but I really do believe we should have that choice. The decision could be included in a living will.

## That's life

I don't know whether it is me or whether the world is really going to crazy? I just read an article in the newspaper about 'Empathy Suit' or 'Mobility-Restriction Suit' and even 'Age Simulation Suit'. Basically, care professionals, including doctors, are meant to wear these in a training situation so they get an idea of what life is like for an old person. I think it is dreadful. What ever happened to old fashioned care or asking the patient? Is this a 'cheapskate' and quicker way of finding out how an old person feels? Will they be pretending to be children or pregnant women next?

Another thing that annoyed me was when my friend received a letter when she was 70 to say that she would no longer be sent a letter asking her to have a mammogram - apparently funding for this stops at 70. The letter said she could phone after 3 years and make an appointment but she wouldn't be notified that one was due. Yet I read that a man who was 74 was going to have an operation to help his sex life. Is it better to have a good sex life or to die of cancer? Clearly someone in government has decided on priorities!

Whilst I'm having a moan, I'll carry on! Older people get sent a pack to use to test for bowel cancer – poo sticks I call them! I have enough difficulty using them and putting them back in their place to send off, not to mention the indignity of trying to use them, but what about the people who aren't quite as agile as I am?....and the writing of the instructions is so small that you almost need a magnifying glass to read. It's the same on some packaging and jars where, even if I hold the thing to the light, I can hardly read them so I just guess. Perhaps the people who produce these things should wear an 'Empathy Suit'?

Some of the headlines we read in papers really annoy me. I just saw one that said the government was in a panic because of the explosion of the aging population. What that really means is that they haven't planned for the services to cope with people who are living longer or put enough money into the pot. I bet that we will be called on to pay for more and more. They have already increased the age when people can receive their State pension to 68. I wonder what other plans they have? Pensions are already adjusted if you stay in hospital and you only have a few weeks grace when going into a care home before having to pay for your care.

The whole question of money is a big problem. I know some people tried changing the name on the deeds of their house to their family's name in order to avoid paying for care later on. The law changed and now the old people have had to pay solicitors to put it back as it was. In some cases they had to pay a fine. Emer, someone who works in a charity shop with me, said that her neighbour became thinner and thinner. Apparently he was not eating properly as his family was keeping him short of money having offered to help him manage his money. From what I hear, there is quite a lot of that about – people trying to hold onto their inheritance.

Mental health is another major problem as you get older. I remember my father-in-law really went crazy. We would get calls in the middle of the night in December from his neighbours saying that he was out in the street in his vest and pants, or that he was trying to smash down his front door with an axe. We tried very hard to get the various mental health services to act but without success. The neighbours sometimes called the police but by the time they arrived, he would be fine so they went away again. He would often ring us during the night too for no obvious reason. Eventually my niece said she would have his calls diverted to her house so we could get a night's sleep. One night for her was enough. She suggested that we divert all the calls to the mental health social worker. Amazingly, within 24 hours we had all the services we felt he needed! The social worker also asked why she had been called throughout the night.

The next stage, though, was getting past the psychologist who thought we wanted my father-in-law taken into a hospital or a home so we could sell his house and get the money. What she hadn't bothered to check was that the house already belonged to the family.

I was talking to a friend recently about this dreadful time when people get dementia or Alzheimer's. She then mentioned a super book by Tony Husband (Take Care, Son, published by Little, Brown Book Group). It is about is father Ron who suffered from dementia. When Ron Husband started to forget things - dates, names, where he'd put things - it took a while for his family to realise that this was a different kind of forgetting - it was the first sign of the dementia. Now his illustrator son, Tony, has turned their story into a heartbreaking picture book. The result is a fabulous account that certainly struck a chord with me - so many of his illustrations could have been my father-in-law. There are things in this book that we didn't even realise were mental health issues. I couldn't stop reading it.

Here are a few captions that go with pictures in the book.

*'Hi ... it's us.'*   'Come to get my money, I bet. Well you're not having it.'

**We contacted social services who, it must be said, were very good.**

'I had my car taken off me. My independence was being eroded bit by bit. I felt isolated, lost...'   'We had no choice, Dad. You were a liability on the roads'.

*Quick give me a hand ... that old guy's left his handbrake off!'*

'I've not seen my family in months, you know.'   *'They're in the back room ... they've been with you all day, love.'*

And finally

I remember one time, though. I'd spent a few hours with you in your room. You slept, I worked. Then, when I left and said goodbye, you replied, clear as a bell: 'Take care son.' It took me aback. They were the last words I heard you say.

*It was like a candle flickering back to life for a moment ... then it went out for ever.*

**Part 5**

**There to help!**

As people age, they often need regular help from other people to make their lives tolerable. This might be physical or mental help or just someone to visit for a chat. Neighbours may call in or bring the odd meal to someone; family may come if they live sufficiently close by; social services often have the task of organising support both by using paid care staff or volunteers.

I think it is important to help the person to maintain their independence for as long as possible, whether or not they live alone and/or with a family - regardless of age. One London borough has, I think, organised a brilliant service arranging contact between older people and young people.

This came from a young single parent who was a care leaver who lived in a block of flats. Below her lived a widowed older lady who initially was a little shy about offering her help outright so started by baking a few cakes and giving them to the girl and her child. This gradually increased until the woman was making them all a Sunday roast. What this meant was that the lady was getting company, feeling needed and helping in a most practical way. The care leaver was getting company; someone to talk to and seek advice from. The lady was acting like a grandmother to the child including doing babysitting and in return was getting help with the heavy shopping and with some chores. It was mutually beneficial to both the adults and to the child. I think someone should organise this nationwide.

I use as many of the services offered to me as I can though I am going to have to get used to using them even more now I can't drive. I use my bus pass, particularly if I am in London visiting family/friends. I have a train pass too which gives me at least a third off train fares. There are also lots of discounts such as for cinema and theatre tickets. Get out and enjoy life I say. I know it's not as easy for everyone who perhaps might not have much money, but the bus pass is perfect as it doesn't cost anything to you. All our buses are full of 'senior citizens' who if they didn't get out might be a social problem to themselves and others or be very lonely. I hope no government ever tries to take away our bus passes.

Many people who have been in responsible jobs during their working life decide, when they retire, to offer their services as volunteers to help older people. Others who have not worked also do a lot of volunteering particularly for the elderly. This can be helping someone who has lost their sight to live as normal a life as possible; visiting an elderly person who has no family and might see no-one but the volunteer; serving food at day centres for the elderly; driving a minibus for outings for older people or to collecting and delivering donations of furniture and fittings for a charity. The tasks are endless and so too are the volunteers. I just heard about this ex-headmaster who fits elastic stockings. I'm not sure I would cope with a guy coming to do that but he does seem very popular. However, it seems to me that some charities do not respect the volunteers the way they should and the volunteers seem to be treated as second class citizens.

I read in the paper that the health problems and mortality rates of older people are far worse in depressed areas. Perhaps we should harness some of these many volunteers that we hear about and get them volunteering in depressed areas rather than, say, doing one afternoon a week in the local middle class charity shop?

My friend's father was, to all intents and purposes, fine until the local pub closed down. "I can't remember a day since I was born when he didn't go to the pub for one or two pints." she said. After his wife died and he had retired, the pub became even more important to him as a way of engaging with people. As his hearing deteriorated, going to the pub was still great as he could sit and laugh and be with people. I am sure it was more or less straight away after the pub closure that he started going downhill. His health deteriorated and his brain went too. The pub may have been a commercial organisation but it was the lifeline for the lonely old chap. It's much the same with the closure of some of the day-centres and luncheon clubs for the elderly. The people don't go for the food necessarily - though it does ensure they get a decent meal - but for the company and camaraderie. My next door neighbour said that as soon as her mother stopped playing bowls she started to go downhill and died not long afterwards – there must be a moral here.

As people age they start to be less mobile than they used to be, older people are often given aids to help them such as Zimmer frames, walking sticks, a crutch and even electric buggies, though sometimes they have to buy/hire these buggies themselves. What doesn't happen, it seems to me, is that anyone really shows the person how to use the equipment properly, or if they do, they get one quick lesson, which if, they are like me they won't remember. Perhaps this is something volunteers could do?

Someone who used to go to our day centre went to live in a warden assisted home and hired an electric buggy – no test required! She damaged two cars at the home whilst driving the buggy and was also brought back by the police several times as she was driving dangerously. Eventually, the home said that she couldn't keep the buggy there, which in reality meant she couldn't keep her buggy. She was very upset by this but her family were relieved. She used the money instead to get a taxi to take her to the supermarket, hairdressers or chiropodist. Who knows, but perhaps it was all the drugs she was taking that made her drowsy and so drive badly?

Hearing aids are another problem for some people. Just when their dexterity deteriorates they are given the most intricate piece of equipment which goes into their ear and needs the tiniest of batteries to make it work. One brief lesson is all they get. I know I went round to see my neighbour several times to help her with her hearing aid but in the end she gave in and stopped using it.

There are lots of other hearing aids available, such as loops in shops and churches so long as people remember to switch them on and the person with the hearing problem knows how to, or is able to, switch their hearing aid to 'loop' setting.

# There to help!

When my father-in-law started to go deaf he had terrible trouble trying to use a hearing aid as his fingers were so enormous and calloused from years of working outside on the land. When, aged, 83, he found a 'lady friend' aged 93 who was also deaf the outcome was often ridiculous. On one occasion, she said to him 'Would you like a Murray Mint?' to which he replied 'Marry you, why on earth would I want to marry you?

My youngest sister is now totally deaf. She's only in her 70's but her hearing has not been very good since the War. She was very close to a building when a bomb went off. The noise damaged her hearing which has got much worse recently. She's always coped and now she is the 'fastest texter in town'! Her family bought her a mobile phone and showed her how to text. Now she uses text messaging all the time. She and her friend are in constant touch several times a day sending messages to each other. The internet and web have also been an absolute boon for her. Her grandchildren send her texts and e mails and she knows all the latest news without having to buy a newspaper.

Emer was talking the other day, during our coffee break at the charity centre where we both help, about how she met her husband. She was saying, when she was younger, she went for an interview to do the accounts at a religious brotherhood in Ireland. When she went home she told her mother that the brother who had interviewed her was 'absolutely gorgeous'. Her mother gave her a very strict dressing down explaining that once a brother always a brother. Emer got the job and the rest is history. In 2015 Emer and Larry have been married 50 years.

How romantic – leaving the brotherhood for love! Here is Larry's story:

*I was born in a little village, Drangan in County Tipperary on 8th August 1935. There was another child in the village called John Joe Clancy (known as JJ) who was born on the same day. The tradition in Ireland is that you are baptised the next day after your birth, which means the mother is not at the baptism. I was born at home. At the baptism we were mixed up and if it wasn't for JJ's father I would have had the wrong name – he realised in the nick of time that the priest had the wrong child!*

*I was the youngest of 6 children. All my family are dead now except my sister who was 80 in June 2013.*

*We had a small farm, 16 Irish acres, which is about 22 normal acres! We had a cow and sent milk to the creamery. We used to grow beet and all our own potatoes and vegetables. My father also had to work as there was not enough income from the farm. He was a War veteran. He had served with the Cheshire regiment and fought in the trenches in the 1914 –18 War eventually being posted to Thessalonica in Greece in 1916 until the end of the War. He was then posted to India but I don't think he went - but he certainly did have Malaria and got really bad doses. I used to sit by his bed watching him as a kid. It is quite terrifying what Malaria does to people. I left to go to Dublin in December 1949 and he left this earth 3 months later at the age of 56, so I never saw him again.*

*At the age of 4, I started infant's school in the convent. At first my sisters took me. Later, reluctantly I took JJ to*

# There to help!

*school because he was very shy. We used to walk 2½ miles each way. When JJ started school he created and screamed and ran away. I was chasing him and begging him to come back. Eventually he settled in. I stayed with the nuns until I was 7 or 8 then went to the boys' school until I was nearly 14. The teacher had a cane, a little ash one which was round and because he smoked so much it was all yellow. We only had him for a few weeks because he got killed on a bike. He was at the races and coming back down the hill he fell off his bike.*

*When I was 13, a friend told me he had been to the convent to see the sister about becoming a brother of the Saint of God Hospitaller. He said he was keen to do it. He said it was a nursing order of brothers and it served people with psychiatric problems. It was on the way home from school that he told me about it and asked if I would come too. I said why not. He took me in to see the sister and she said "I don't believe it." I was a bit wild when I was younger, always doing some sport or activity, so she was surprised. She did all the organising and a brother from the order came down to see us and then the forms came for us to fill in. I remember distinctly the forms said 'Why do you want to become a religious brother?' So I asked my father, a very impatient man, what to put and he said "For God I suppose." All the applications went off. This was June or July, the brothers said I was too young because I was only 13 but I wrote back and told them I would be 14 in August.*

*So we went up to Dublin on a train to join the brothers. This was my first time on a train – the old smoking engine. I remember my father saying to me before we left, "Be careful, don't put your head out of the window you never know about the smoke or the bridges." These were the very last words he said to me.*

*So we joined. We were called aspirants; there were about 20 of us and we had a brother in charge. We went to school to Monks Town College run by the Christian brothers. The very first day in school they put up on the board sums in algebra and I had never heard of algebra in my whole life. The brother was disgusted, he almost hit me with the cane but realised I wasn't joking. I wasn't good at Maths but good at English and Latin.*

*How strict it was for us aspirants. It was an all male environment. We couldn't have a particularly close friendship. If you got on too well with another boy they split you up in case you became sexually attracted - there was a lot of it around!*

*We went through the school for 3 years and I did the intermediate certificate but I didn't do the leaving certificate because, at 17, I went into the postulate to prepare for the brotherhood. I was a year doing that in plain clothes and then after a year you became a novice and was given a habit - the long black robe with a cowl which you pulled over your head. You remained a novice for 2 years. In the meantime as a postulate and as a novice we were training to be nurses and we had a tutor several times a week where we learned physiology and all the things to do as a nurse. Interestingly, the book on the full range of nursing that we were given contained all the different parts of the body except the reproductive system. This had been torn out as we were not allowed to see that.*

## There to help!

*We then made our first profession which was called 'the simple profession' where you dedicated yourself to God. This wasn't permanent as you had the choice of leaving until you were 24 if you changed your mind. So at 24 we made our solemn profession which was permanently dedicating our lives to the religious order - which I did with a number of others on 2nd July 1959. When I got the habit I took the name Brother Albert. Between my simple profession and the solemn one we had qualified as psychiatric nurses. I was sent to a place called Celbridge in County Kildare where they had adults with severe special needs and I spent some time there. When you were on duty you fed them, did everything for them and stayed with them over night. I was there a year. I had one very traumatic incident. There was a boy admitted who was hydrocephalus (large head). I said goodbye to his parents, then took him up to where he was going to sleep. I was unpacking his case and I sat him on a stool as there was no chair. Being naive, I didn't realise he was top heavy and he fell over and cracked his skull. He didn't die - but he did die young.*

*At this time my mother ran the farm and I had to go to see her when I was still in the brotherhood. I said she should hand the farm over to my brother, as he had said he couldn't get married whilst mother was running the farm. She did pass it on eventually. Then he got married and he subsequently had 12 children. My mother then, sort of gave up, she had no interests, and died when she was 76. My brother's wife still lives on the farm.*

*I spent some time in Drumcar in County Louth, which is on the border with Northern Ireland and here there were even more severely 'special needs' people. The average IQ was about 50. There were adults and children in other units and I was in charge of a children's unit.*

*Some of them who were diagnosed as special needs were in fact autistic and we had a programme where we had them assessed at the recently opened child guidance clinic in Rathgar, Dublin. This was run by the brothers who had employed psychiatrists, psychologists, social workers and speech therapists. Some of these children were sent to this clinic and they got the help they needed – we were slowly becoming a bit more enlightened. Most of the patients were severely disabled. We took some visitors around one time and they became extremely distressed and traumatised and started to cry - I had to take them outside.*

*I was then made the bursar and was in that role for about a year. I had a secretary who also did the books and I had to make sure they were OK. After a period of time they decided to send me to the child guidance clinic in Dublin so I acted as secretary there. All the people who came for assessment or treatment were children with their parents. I would have to organise who they saw and make the appointments. The parents saw the social worker, who took their whole history. She had sheets and sheets of facts. We had a whole cross section of society from the wealthy to the poor who all had problematic children. I was there about 18 months and then came back to the original place as bursar. I was quite popular everywhere but when I went back to Stillorgan the head psychiatrist said, "I hear you have been doing good work everywhere and we hope we will get the same work out of you here," or something to that effect.*

# There to help!

*Being bursar was a big job because I had to send out all the bills for all the patients who were in-patients. We had a lot of priests with drug, psychiatric and/or sexual problems. A lot of these priests had come back from missions in Africa. One priest I remember was lovely, but daft. He was parish priest in Dublin and he gave everything away to the poor who probably tricked him. The bank wrote to the archbishop to say that the priest owed a lot of money – thousands. The priest said he would just write a cheque. They then realised that he was mentally ill and put him in John of Gods.*

*The psychologist who was employed in child guidance was sent to America for more experience. When he came back he had to get all his employment issues sorted so he got a taxi in Dublin and they took him to the American Embassy, Canadian Embassy, Ministry of Health plus the Psychology Department of University College, Dublin. He then got the taxi back. He said "We are finished, now take me to John of Gods" so the taxi driver thought he was mad and kept him under observation all the way there.*

*I may have put some events out of sequence because I spent a year in Obelisk Park, Blackrock - a school for the more gifted special needs children. We had a very forward thinking Prior who organised lots of activities including operettas and pantomimes. These attracted people from the Dublin theatres who acted with the boys.*

*It must have come for my time to solemnly profess at the age of 24 – you lie on the floor with your hands out. It was a very solemn occasion and all the family were there. After this I was still bursar but my other duty in the hospital was the PR side. I had to meet the bishops who came to see their priests and ensure they got their tea and cakes and also to provide a sitting room for them. The Archbishop of Dublin was extremely right wing and would not allow any Catholics to attend Trinity College, a protestant institution. He was a good friend of the Prime Minister and in those years the government bowed to the church. When the Archbishop came to see his priests, I used to take him to see them and he made sure the seating was arranged so that the priest he was visiting had all the light focused on the priest's face and the Archbishop sat in the shade so they couldn't see his thinking but he could see their thinking and body language.*

*Around the time of my solemn profession, we had a tutor in to help me get the matriculation and leaving certificate as they thought I should go to university. We had a year with a tutor who got 4 or 5 of us through – equivalent to 'A' levels.*

*At some point, I was also sent to Glasgow to Jordon Hill College for 6 months learning how to teach children with disabilities, both mental and physical. Most of the children - with physical needs particularly - were highly intelligent children and I got a certificate showing that I could teach them. I was then asked to go to the child guidance clinic for 3 months where I learned 'play therapy'. I stayed with a wonderful family. I was 8 stone when I arrived and 13 stone when I left. The lady fed me 3 large meals a day. I met some lovely people and went to see the football teams. I had a free seat at Parkhead (Celtic Football ground) because I wore a clerical collar – Catholic churchmen no longer get that treatment. I really enjoyed Glasgow. I was*

# There to help!

*called back rather suddenly by telephone as they obviously thought I was enjoying too much freedom! We then had the elections which are held every 3 years for the various officers and I was elected as Prior of the child guidance services so I effectively became the manager of the child guidance clinic in Dublin. Whilst there, I went to the university 3/4 nights a week on my motorbike. The University was a new experience for me as I met a whole variety of people. As well as doing my job as Prior and studying, I was teaching 3 or 4 children a day for an hour each. That ceased when we opened a school and I was headmaster of the school for a year. It was decided that really we ought to have an outside person to build it up from about 10 children to a really thriving school. I was paid by the Department of Education for the headmastership.*

*The very first evening I went to university we were sitting in this big hall, the lecturer was known as a heavy drinker, he stood in front of us and was a bit unsteady on his feet but was very lucid. He said "We are doing the whole range of English literature. Forget everything you learned at school - none of it is relevant for a university degree." I got my BA in 1965.*

*Our system at work in the clinic was that we had 2 men who came in to do the typing for the psychiatrists but we needed someone to do the bookkeeping. The inspector for schools used to come to inspect us and as we were chatting I told him I was looking for a bookkeeper and secretary. He said "My son's girlfriend is just back from France and needs a job." That was Emer (who later became my wife) and we took her on. When Emer came the first day for interview there was a brother who answered the door and she said "Could I see Brother Albert" and he said "I am him." She was disgusted as he was a very strange man. Anyway I happened to come into the room and he had to change his story.*

*Emer was not really sure she could do the work as there were so many ledgers but I persuaded her to give it a try. She stayed 18 months and that's how our relationship formed. When we got too close I applied to leave. They tried really hard to get me to change my mind. The brother, a lovely kindly man, did tell me later that he hoped I would change my mind as he felt that my leaving might affect many of the younger brothers. The brothers said they would write to Rome – to clear my leaving but they didn't do it. Twice they promised but didn't do it. That was summer of 1965.*

*I then I went to see them again and they asked me to see a doctor. He said*

*"Are you sure?"*

*Then he said "How strong is it and how much sexual desire do you have?"*

*I said "Pretty good"*

*He said "It should be 75% sexual."*

*I said "Well yes, that is really the case."*

## There to help!

*They then got the clearance from the doctor and as I had a solemn profession they did write to Rome to get permission for me to leave.*
*My mother wasn't very happy when I took Emer down to see her and said I was leaving. My brother tried to convince me not to leave the order until my mother died and I said I couldn't. She was very upset because an Irish mother is very proud of any one with a clerical collar. A lot of the priests they used to say "the mother had the vocation".*

*We decided to get married and then Emer went to tell her family. I knew them as I had often been to her home. Emer said to her family that Brother Albert wants to get married and her father said "I wish him well." but she said "Dad, Brother Albert wants to marry me." He accepted it. I think he probably knew deep down. I used to dress in lay clothes when I went out with Emer though I wasn't meant to.*

*The brothers gave me permission and money to buy all the lay clothes I needed and they arranged for me to be measured at Clery's store in Dublin for my clothes. They were a very caring order of brothers unlike some other religious orders who more or less abandoned those who left the religious life. They also gave me £300 which in 1966 was very generous. I used to go to Emer's house on a Sunday morning and I met her brother and he helped me write letters for jobs in England – I knew too many people in Dublin and thought it would be better to go away for a couple of years.*

*We got married in Dublin and came across to Emer's sister's house. They had gone away so we had it to ourselves for a week. Then I came to Southampton for job interviews as a social worker. Roger Tilly was head of the children's department. I was seen by the officers and, later, I was taken across to the Civic Centre to meet the chair of the Children's Committee, who happened to be the mother of the late John Stonehouse, renowned as the person who faked his death in America. They interviewed me in this huge room, I can't remember all the questions Mrs Stonehouse asked me, but I do I remember her saying "We (Southampton Football Club) are only in the $2^{nd}$ division at the moment but aim to get to the $1^{st}$ division, will you be supporting us?". I said "Absolutely." and got the job!*

*So I started in the children's department. We stayed in a B&B in Hill Lane, and then we looked around for a suitable flat to rent which took some time. My salary was £1010 pounds per year. We had two children so had to change flats a couple of times. However, we had some luck. 1971 was the year of the census and we both got jobs with the census which we did in the evenings. Emer was in charge, I just went round collecting. We nearly made enough money for a deposit to buy the house we live in now. We were £100 short so Emer contacted her mum and dad and they sent her the £100. Our third child arrived within a year of moving into our new house.*

*I retired in 1997 and subsequently did several other projects for Hampshire County Council including setting up the mentoring scheme for young people leaving care, in which Prince Charles had a specific interest. Whenever we* took young people to the Prince's Trust offices in London, the Prince took them aside and spent much time with them discussing their problems. I also did some work looking at the priorities in child protection cases and writing chronologies of young people in care. I also chaired the fostering panel for a private foster care company and spent 11 years there. This stopped in 2011.

Life as a brother was very hard especially when I was young as the work involved long hours including night watch. However, I think that the Brotherhood, probably, due to the nature of the work they did, was very caring and concerned for our well-being. Although leaving the brothers was a huge step to take it did not destroy my Christian beliefs. We still keep in touch with the brothers from the time to time and have been invited there for special events. Emer and I went back for their centenary celebrations. I have no regrets about leaving the brotherhood to marry Emer.

----ooOoo----

How romantic – leaving the brotherhood for love!

Although Larry left the brotherhood to marry Emer, he has always cared for people – in his role as social worker and in his personal life. Aged, 79 now, he still helps people less fortunate than himself but particularly older people. His life has always been about caring for others.

**Part 6**

**From cradle to grave**

When we have our own children we are often under pressure from our parents, family and friends to conform and to have our children follow their faith – even have a ceremony of that faith, such as baptism. I certainly had Patsy christened for that reason. It was also a bit of an excuse to get everyone together so they could admire my new daughter. Sadly, for me it had no meaning and I still have a bit of a conscience about that even now.

My mother got remarried some years after my father died. During the ceremony at the local registry office, the registrar asked for my father's death certificate. My mother didn't have it, assuming they would have it as she had registered my father's death there. The whole ceremony was stopped whilst the registrar went down into the vaults and came up 10 minutes later with the certificate. The ceremony continued. There must be a moral here about assumptions!

Over the years I've been to various ceremonies such as weddings, blessings and naming ceremonies. There have also been parties to celebrate specific birthdays such as $60^{th}$, $70^{th}$ and so on. I was at a $60^{th}$ party once when the 'birthday boy' was absolutely livid that a surprise party had been arranged for him and even more livid when he saw who the guest of honour was! I vowed then that I would never ever get involved with a surprise party, but I have ensured a good celebration for all my special events.

For my 50th I decided to learn to windsurf which was hilarious as I managed to fall off over 40 times before succeeding in sailing the thing up and down the lake once – the aim of the course. I then fell in again and slowly, exhausted, dragged the surf board back to the side of the lake where my friends were in fits of laughter watching me - they had given up long ago. For my 60th I rode my bike 60 miles for 60 years in the London to Brighton annual cycle ride and for my 70th I learnt to 'drive' a speed boat and also did several other things including having a party for 60 friends.

Patsy didn't make Jane take part in any sort of birth or naming ceremony. In fact when Patsy re-married she had a Humanist ceremony where they have a celebrant and you and they work out the ceremony you want to have. Humanists as far as I can see believe in the 10 commandments but without the God bit, which I agree with. In fact I have written down that when I die I want to have a Humanist funeral. I want to have my funeral in the woodlands close by and to be buried in a cardboard coffin. I also want people to have a great party afterwards to celebrate my life, which, overall, I would say has been pretty good.

When a partner of many years dies, it can be really traumatic. One of the things about old age is that you gradually spend more and more time together with your partner so when the loss occurs the loneliness can be overwhelming. I might be wrong but men seem to struggle with being on their own, outwardly at least, more than women. I was in the doctor's recently and a man came into the waiting room where his wife was sitting.

She asked him if he had his prescription, if he needed the toilet and then told him to put his coat on – she helped him do this too. He seemed perfectly capable to making all these decisions but just shrugged and did as he was told. Perhaps it is because women naturally seem to nurture children, so when the children are gone they turn their attention to their partners who, earlier in their life, may have been 'spoilt' by their mothers so go along with being spoilt again. When they are on their own they then have to look after themselves which often comes as quite a shock.

I saw a Facebook post, from Bob, which shows that Bob's wife was still concerned for Bob's welfare even as she was dying.

*This is the evening of the worst day of my family's life. I was asked by the Sister at the Hospice to say to my EVE it is ok, I will be alright. She can go now, because they felt she had looked after me for her entire life but was still worried for me and was holding on for that reason. Cradling her in my arms with tears running down my face and whispering the things your heartbeat wants to hear, and then saying I will be alright and she can leave us now, she took one last breath and passed away in my arms. I still, and will always, love EVE, she was not only my wife and my lovely children's rock but everybody who knew her loved her.*

---ooOoo---

As you get older, death seems to come into our lives more and more. In fact, last year I went to 7 funerals. I know it is something to do with my age but, oh, they were such awful events.

But I must tell you about Betty. I was at the funeral of her husband, my uncle Bobby. It was in Scotland where they have huge wakes where all and sundry seem to turn up for a free meal and drink afterwards. Just before I was leaving to catch my plane back home I went to say good bye. Betty is almost 90 now and a very large lady who doesn't move around very much. She was sitting, with her 18 stone body and her full flowing clothes, on and over a chair! As I sat down and leant towards her, she started to tell me about the day Bobby died. She said she called the undertaker who came to prepare Bobby and put him in his coffin. The undertaker asked Betty for Bobby's teeth which she duly gave him and he put them in Bobby's mouth. The next morning Betty realised that she had given the undertaker her own false teeth and kept Bobby's. She immediately 'phoned the undertaker who said he would do his best to remove the teeth from the now rigid body, which he did, and brought them back to Betty. She thanked him and gave him Bobby's teeth. She washed her teeth and put them in her own mouth. "You see Alice, I dinna want to waste money on a new pair of teeth at my time of life" she said. I was still laughing when I got back on the plane to go home.

I find it strange how important funerals seem to be for many people. I hear people say things such as 'Oh, a lovely send off' and 'Oh, didn't they do him proud?' For other people though, funerals are the least important part of life. I know several people who don't go to funerals but do visit the people when they are alive or sick, either in their home, care home or in hospital as the case may be. I like that idea.

Funerals can be very strange. The lady who made my new curtains was telling me that her father had remarried and had become a Jehovah's Witness. When he died she found her father's funeral confusing and not at all comforting. Everything was alien to her.

I know someone who had a Humanist funeral after his father's death. The celebrant was an ex-Church of England vicar who carried out a lovely service except, at the end, as the people were leaving, he somehow reverted back to his old ways by saying 'God Bless'. Fortunately people were amused rather than offended.

Rosie, in her story about her dad, really typifies unwittingly so much about death – it coming, when it happens and what happens afterwards. I met Rosie at one of those awful get-togethers in someone's house to listen to other people sing. Rosie seemed so lonely sitting in the corner on her own. I went over and started to talk to her and that's when her story came out in full flow:

*My mother died in childbirth when I was just three years old. My father was left with 4 children. He was on his own for 9 years. The newborn baby went to live with an aunt for 18 months, and shortly after he came back my older brother went to boarding school. Initially we were cared for at home by various family and friends. We then had 2 housekeepers, the first one was universally hated, and the second one we loved. We were almost as close to her as to a mother. We were very fond of her and kept in touch until her death.*

*After my birth mother died, we moved to Exeter, where my father remarried. When we had all left home, my father and step mother then moved to Bristol (because of my father's job with the bank) where they lived for 34 years. They moved back down to Exeter three years ago to be near my sister and two brothers. I moved away at the age of 18 and have never returned to live in Devon.*

*My father's father was a philanderer. Dad was sent to boarding school and lost both his parents as a teenager. My birth mother was one of 6. My father had just started work in a bank at 18 when he met my mum who came from a huge farming family. He absolutely loved everything about her family; it was wonderful for him.*

*What has been interesting is that so much about my father's life has resurfaced since his death. It took us back to his first marriage and how hugely important it was. The chapel of rest was very close to his first home with my first mother. I have never felt very close to my step mother though to this day I refer to her as mother. I left home at 18 – she married my father when I was 12. I didn't deliberately distance myself from her but have always found it difficult to show her any affection.*

*They met at a friend's house, went to the same church, and then Dad invited her back after church. One day she asked us to call her by her first name. Auntie Edna, our housekeeper, was very helpful in smoothing the way when my father told us he was going to remarry. Apparently, my father needed a lot of persuasion about getting married again.*

*My step mother (Evangeline – we called her Vangie) bought me my first suspender belt and bra, and clothes. She was glamorous so we were also quite pleased as we had a mother who could come to speech days at school. We also inherited another car which we liked!*

*They went on honeymoon to Padstow. We gave them 4 days on their own then us kids and a French exchange student joined them. Vangie did try to have a child of her own but she was 39 by then so it didn't happen. She was quite helpful with boyfriends and things for me and she was quite good, I thought, as a granny, though my older daughter, wrote something which I found - 'maybe 'cos granny never had a child of her own.......' - so perhaps not?*

*I think my father always struggled with the idea of getting old. Before he got old he made jokes about it, even in his late middle age he seemed to have a fear of old age. He didn't embrace getting old; as he got older and frailer I think he found life really difficult. He didn't want to stop driving. He was also worried about my step-mum who was 7 years younger than him. He couldn't be the patriarch of the family. In his late 70's he used to say he didn't want to get old. He started to decline at about 87/88 years. At the same time, mother found being put in the role of carer and responsible person very hard. She had been sort of thrown into these difficult roles.*

*It was a very gentle decline and he didn't want to move from where they had been living before but they moved to a warden assisted apartment before he was 90. We said it* would be the making or breaking of him but the move speeded up his decline.

Was he happy? He always said he was so happy to have his family about him and this became an increasing theme - how much joy he got from seeing them. He said it was good that he moved back to Exeter but we felt it was another step in a journey that he didn't really want to make. My dad cried a lot more as he got older.

My younger brother is on the Aspergers spectrum. He is very good at mending and fixing things; he is also gay which my parents found difficult to cope with. Having said that, my father was obviously very supportive but saddened by it. They didn't approve but they accepted him. My older brother is married with no children and finds it very difficult to express his emotions. He will do anything if asked but won't actively volunteer to help.

My sister got married young, to her one and only boyfriend. She had four children who are all now grown up and living away from home. She has one granddaughter. Both she and her husband were teachers and took early retirement a couple of years ago. They are active in the church that we all used to go to as a family and to which my parents returned to when they moved back to Exeter.

My sister really took on the role of carer of my dad. She already worked with disabled children, so knew how to get dad to do physio and all the practicalities such as using a catheter. I found it difficult and my mother did too. As time went on my stepmother's impatience got worse which we found difficult. To her it was a bit like having a toddler again. She would say, "Have you got your gloves, hankie, hat and stick?" which she had to do and everything took so long. It was a logistical nightmare for her.

I think I got quite upset that my mother didn't seem to do it with patience and care. I'm sure they loved each other. She was trained as a social worker specialising in child protection. Before that she had worked as a nanny. As our mother she was patient, but when it came to caring for dad at the other end of life needing similar care, she struggled. It upset me. I went to see my dad and he would say, "I am in the dog house." Yet he was the kindest man I ever met. Was it to do with being the stepmother?

Dad had a couple of spells in hospital and then after the 2nd spell he went into a rehabilitation hospital. They were very nice people. It was my first experience of such an institution. The clientele were all similar people who just watched tv all the time. I don't want to knock it, but it was a rude awakening. However it became clear that my mother wouldn't cope if dad went back to their home.

When he was in the hospital I took them down to the sea front in Exmouth where we sat in the car and watched the sea. When we got back to the rehab hospital, he had to get back into a wheelchair. Mother insisted she went and got some nurses to help him. I said dad we can do this and he got himself out of the car and helped himself into the wheelchair - Vangie seemed to have given up on him. Another time when my daughter went to see him in hospital he wasn't allowed to go home without going to the loo alone. My mother never encouraged him to do it or to do *his physio. It was almost as though she didn't want him to get better.*

*We had a debate with all the family. My sister and I, particularly my sister, took on the responsibility. So the whole debate came up about what to do. At the time my parents had a 2 bedroom warden assisted place and my father had had people coming in every morning to help him get up. When we talked about what to do with him after leaving rehab my sister and I probably thought mother was being unreasonable. She could have afforded to have someone to live in or give more care. We couldn't accept her decision. She should have done everything possible to make it work but she just wasn't prepared to do it. My family don't do emotion, so we didn't voice our opinions.*

*For a while my sister explored moving him in with her. She was incensed that my mum wanted to move him into a home. The solution was, "Let's look at homes, let's look at costs, then she might make the decision." I did the research, and found he needed a nursing home not a care home.*

*The next thing we found difficult was that my mother went to see a home which was on a bus route as she no longer could drive. That annoyed my sister; it was not about making life easy for her but the best place for dad. Mother didn't want him to go to any other home. That put our backs up a bit. In the end they couldn't take him so the one where he went suited him. It was called 'Woodhayes'. Almost in sight of his old school and he felt like it was his home-coming. It was an old Georgian house with lovely gardens. It felt the right place for him so I think that my* sister felt better. My mother was OK about it but she wouldn't take taxis and as it was not on a bus route she was very dependent on my sister or local friends taking her to see dad.

The other thing that really annoyed me is that she is such a creature of habit, visiting only in the afternoon. She would go every afternoon, even though that was the time when the home organised activities for the residents. She only visited in the afternoon, even though she could have gone all day; even the day he died she left her house in the afternoon.

When he went to the home he settled well and was universally loved because he was always pleasant and polite and made an effort with his carers. They spoke very highly of him. The most bizarre thing was that my mother didn't seem at all interested in making his room like a home. I would say, "Don't you think dad would like a radio or something to play music on?" "No he wouldn't manage it, no he won't want to watch tv." It was bizarre not wanting to help people you love. Everything we suggested she said no. Even her expectations of my father went down.

I suppose there was definitely a sense of relief after he died; I think they are linked in a funny way. One thing I found quite interesting, I always felt pulled to Devon, I felt it is where my roots are and I went down there quite a bit. Now there is part of me that no longer wants to go there. Obviously I will do all I can to help my mother and I am sorting the financial affairs with my brother, but honestly, at the moment I don't feel very close to her. I telephone her *once a week. I do anything she wants out of a sense of duty. She is still in the warden assisted place. I find her quite difficult to help because she is so set in her ways. I made a suggestion to make life easier but she doesn't want to change. She has been quite cold, wants my dad's things out of the flat, out of the way.*

*She was one of 7 children. They had a very strict upbringing. Her family do not visit as they are not nearby, but she has friends she has made where she lives who pop in with bowls of casserole and things. Her health has deteriorated. It's perhaps unfair of us to take it out on her in a way.*

*Another thing since my father died, I always saw them as a couple and my mother did something the other day which so shocked me. She phoned my niece, her granddaughter, and said, "You really have to sort out your child care as you can't expect your mother to come and help you!" My sister has been helping with babysitting – I think she was jealous or something.*

*My sister is now getting quite good at saying no to my mother. My mother hates, it. Sis tells her that patient transport will pick her up and my mother gets really cross. My sister has to keep saying, "You will have to get on with it; I can't keep taking you everywhere". I know all of this is probably her way of grieving - she was married 45 years. I haven't seen her cry once. Her behaviour is probably because she hasn't grieved.*

*When Dad died, 2 carers in the home were with him. We went down to Devon the next day and had a big family meeting. The brilliant thing was my father had planned his whole funeral, hymns and readings, 3 of us spoke but my older brother couldn't do it. I was so pleased my younger brother spoke. 150 people turned up. It was the funeral as he wanted it. I stayed down for a while and the thing that struck me was that the family found it difficult to talk about dad. We all wrote down what we were going to say and sent it round by e mail. I arranged for all the siblings (and their partners) to go out for meal but I couldn't get anyone to talk about dad. My sister and I probably could, yes, but not in front of everyone.*

*Before he died, dad was losing his mind, repeating things a lot and latterly I didn't feel he expressed himself but I did expect him to talk about his faith or his religion. It would be sad if he had started to question his faith because he got a lot out of it in his life. His wife still has her faith.*

*The funeral went off smoothly. An aunt said, "He can't wait to be with Jesus." My father didn't say that. I was quite surprised that he was not very much at peace; his religion didn't seem to bring him any comfort. When there are a lot of people at a funeral of similar mind, it somehow made it unacceptable to be sad, so I found it rather strange as there was no sense of sadness. They somehow felt he was going to a better place though no-one actually expressed that. It made it hard for those grieving; it felt wrong somehow to feel sad.*

*He was buried not cremated. My birth mother is buried in Yeovil. Driving down to the funeral from London I said to my daughters I wanted to go to the grave but we arrived*

*10 minutes after the cemetery closed; then we went back on the way from the funeral. It was very odd as we couldn't find the grave. My older daughter said, "Well mum, the reason you can't find it is because granddad is so busy catching up with grandma". If you do have that faith and go to heaven how does that make your second wife feel?*

*For me, the funeral brought up a lot of reminiscences from my first mother's family. Then I had a dream – I don't particularly believe my parents are together – but I woke up one morning in floods of tears. It occurred to me that my mother was up there telling my father what I had got up to. I cried a lot when I got the news of my father's death but don't think I have cried since. My middle name is Joy and dad used to say it is such a joy to see you. Having said that, my sister and I still speak on the 'phone to have rants to each other about the rest of the family.*

*I have 2 children; one tells me absolutely everything and asks for advice, the other one is so private and won't talk. My husband still struggles within the family, with expressing his needs but he is much better than me at understanding the girls.*

*Somehow, I have no voice, I can't express my needs. I think my step mother is quite similar.*

----ooOoo----

Rosie seems to have anger, bitterness, blame, someone to blame, love, resentment; a whole myriad of emotions with which she is struggling to come to terms. Rosie is also in grave danger of falling out with her (step) mother, probably when her mother needs her the most, yet she too cannot express or show her emotions.

Death is a funny thing. Some people prepare for it and have all their plans made. Other people go along as though it might never happen.

My nephew, who travels a lot with his job, asked his father all the questions about the type of funeral etc he wanted. At first his father was a little worried and loath to answer but when Jack explained that as he was the only child and was often out of the country it was better if these things could be planned for in advance. He said he didn't want anyone else having to do all these things as it was important to him that he made all provisions for his dad personally. When his dad died, as it happens, he was in the country but the whole process was really easy and allowed him to grieve naturally without worrying about all sorts of practical things. Even the flowers and type of coffin had been chosen and a funeral bond was in place which covered the cost of everything. I keep meaning to get Patsy to organise one for me but then we are not a family who are very good at talking about things, a bit like Rosie really.

I suppose it would be a good idea to say what I wanted doing with all my things. I've made a will, though I don't imagine there will be much money left if Patsy has to sell my house to pay for me if I have to go into one of those care homes or have carers come in to help me. I was thinking about my jewellery, nick knacks and furniture. I'm not sure that there is much that anyone would want, but I would like my grandchildren, nieces and nephews to have some small reminder of me.

I think the strangest thing about death though is the way the person who is directly bereaved seems to always fall out with someone really close to them. Take Grace for example, she had been best friends with Trudy all her life, ever since they were in primary school. After Trudy's daughter died of cancer Trudy wouldn't speak to Grace who just could not understand it. The only thing she could think of was that she, Grace, didn't go to the funeral, but Grace is over 80 and the funeral was in the South of France in the middle of winter. It still worries her to this day. She often says "I don't know why Trudy didn't understand that it would have been too much for me to go all that way on my own." I know of other people who have fallen out with their brothers or sisters and even their mothers and fathers for no obvious reason. It's as though they want to have someone to blame but it is very hard for the person on the receiving end.

After talking to Rosie I've spent a lot of time thinking about death and then I was shown this post from a keen motorcyclist who had written on the XRB motor cycle forum website. I think it says it all.

My hardest post
My wife of 24 years has died.

*We had the flu. That sounds so \*\*\*\*ing stupid....flu.*
*She was so bad last Sunday that she stayed in bed, I made her drinks but she had no appetite and did not eat. The Monday morning I helped her to the toilet and she*

*passed out. I was concerned but not overly worried; she came to almost straight away. I was going to call an ambulance but she wanted just to go to the doctor. At the doctors she collapsed again and an ambulance took her to local hospital. She was put on a drip, had colour back and was laughing at my feeble jokes and annoyed at the inconvenience of being in hospital. I went home to walk the dogs and have my dinner about 6 that evening. All was well.*

*Tuesday when I arrived at the hospital she was in pain, she had not slept and couldn't get comfortable. During the day it got worse. She was moved to a single room and the influenza virus was confirmed. The pain increased and her breathing worsened, pain killers were not helping and she was moved to intensive care to monitor everything better. She asked me to go home to walk the dogs; she was in the best hands. At 9 the hospital rang to say she had gone into arrest and they had had to resuscitate, they were moving her to the University Hospital about 40 minutes away. On arrival they had to re-animate again and I should call a friend. They could not stabilize her and the life support machines were switched off at 07:30 Wed morning.*

*My world, my life, my love has been ripped apart.*

*I need to find the strength to carry on. Always one step further.*

*I am so overwhelmed with the support, PMs, text messages and phone calls from forum friends. I cannot thank you enough for helping me and being there for me.*

*I have the funeral at 13:00 Sat 9th that will be 12 noon UK, please rev your engines loud and long wherever you may be and return to your loved ones safe and hug them. Hug them and tell them you love them.*

*Thank you all, Thank you.*

----ooOoo----

Nick got his wishes. Hundreds of motorcyclists met up and revved their engines as requested. A video was made of some of the motorcyclists as they hooted which was sent to Nick - he lives in Germany and had been in the forces and met his wife when stationed there.

*"Grief is the price we pay for love"*

The Queen of England said that at Princess Diana's funeral. It was probably written for her but nevertheless it is as poignant now as it was then.

The subject of death and how we cope is one of my hobby horses. I don't think we talk about these things enough both before the event and during the grieving process. It seems to me that when someone dies there are no rules for grieving, everyone grieves in a different way; in a way that suits them. When I was young everyone wore black for ages after someone died. In fact I remember my grandfather asking if it was OK for him to not wear his black tie which he had worn since his wife's death ages before. He was going to a wedding and thought it might not be appropriate. Of course, he was right and I had no problem with it but some people did – very strange. Nowadays people wear pink, or yellow or whatever colour they want to wear to remember the person who has died. People have 'celebration of life' ceremonies; huge parties or just nothing after the ceremony - whatever is appropriate to them.

I think people need to be open about the issue of death. They may have regrets about not saying goodbye, about not attending the funeral or even the thoughts and feelings they had about the person before the death. Many people need to talk about their feelings and bereavement counselling does seem to help some people. However, it seems to me that there are far too many counsellors of dubious quality. I heard that they sometimes become emotionally involved with their client which I think is totally out of order.

There is no right way to grieve as far as I can see. Different people react to death in different ways – these may be to cry, go for long walks alone, hide in a crowd and carry on as if nothing had happened, be angry, eat too much or too little, smoke or drink alcohol to excess. Sometimes just talking to friends or family helps though many men do find it hard to talk to anyone so bottle up their grief only for it to come out much later in their life. Memories of the death seem to come back again and again – at birthdays, anniversaries, at Christmas and holiday times, births or other deaths of close friends or family or when we least expect it say whilst watching a film or a play. It doesn't get any easier I can tell you having lost two men with whom I was very close.

One thing that does help some people is symbolism. I remember when my mother died; I spent the day of the funeral in a state of limbo, not able to settle or knowing what to do as I was not going to the service. Eventually, Charles suggested that I should buy a rose bush to plant in my garden in memory to my mother. We bought a bush and chose a 'Peace' rose which had been my mother's favourite when she was alive. The amazing thing was, that once we had planted the rose I felt totally calm and at peace with myself.

Different people grieve in different ways, some people weep and wail, others go quiet and become introverted, others outwardly carry on as though nothing has happened. Grieving is also different in different circumstances. For instance, my nephew died in a sudden tragic accident. His parents were hysterical, moving to being verbose and then, following help, to realizing that the pain won't go away but learning some coping strategies that might help.

It is also very difficult for the parent to cope when an adult son or daughter dies. Take my aunt. Her son was a severe alcoholic and died from failure of his liver when my aunt was 83. Despite all the problems my aunt had experienced with her son over the years, she still loved him and blamed herself for not doing enough to help him.

Loneliness is one of the major problems after the death of a loved one. If a couple have been together years or just a short time the void that is left is intolerable. If it is the death of a child the sound of a child laughing or messing about can haunt the parent of that child and can cause loneliness. When Charles died and I was on my own I was really worried how I was going to cope; when Eddie died I had nursed him for a long time so had become close to him in another way. In both cases, however, I was extremely lonely for ages afterwards.

As part of the grieving process of Nick, he decided to motorcycle around China. Unfortunately, he had a crash and couldn't continue. Instead he is home and has decided to write on Facebook how he feels now about his wife's death. His eulogy says it all.....

*I've thought long and hard about posting here.*
*Part of me has always wanted to but I'm private, preferring to hide my feelings and emotions in the ignorance of those who don't know me or are not part of a close relationship any more. With them you can laugh and pretend everything is OK and forget the pain burning inside for a while.*

*It's my wedding anniversary, 25 years ago I took Silke's hand and promised till death do us part. I didn't realise the impact of that promise.*
*Like most relationships we had our ups and downs and I tried to part on a couple of occasions. The bond of that promise was too strong and I couldn't be away from her. She was hard to live with sometimes but it's so much harder living without her. I've tried over the last 16 months to cope; one of the easiest ways is to ride (on his motorbike). Long distances, long hours.*

*I'm not religious but I've had many moments during my travels thinking that decades, centuries ago people with problems would go to church and seek help. Some would go further and find sanctuary in a monastery to confront the problems and face them with prayer or meditation until they had gone and the person can feel strong enough to leave and continue a life.*

*My motorcycle is my monastery, my helmet my temple. Locked in a shell I've been forced to confront my feelings. They can be blocked and pushed to one side but like a song that won't leave your head they return to torment you until you deal with them to the end and the final chord strikes to let them leave.*

*My bereavement started in a hospital where I had to leave Silke, her fight for life was over, a painful and frightening fight and I couldn't help her, I couldn't protect her, I couldn't fight her assailant. I could only stand there to watch and cry. I still cry.*

*I'm supposed to be in China now, riding the Silk Road, heading for the coast and Hong Kong. I thought and hoped it would be fitting for our anniversary. Instead I'm back home early. I crashed and fell hard breaking my collarbone in the northern China mountains. The rules and regulations in China are strict and without a guide you cannot travel by vehicle. I had to leave the group and stay in hospital for the operation to fixate the bone.*
*And so I've made a full circle. What started in hospital I've tried to leave in hospital. I walked into an operating theatre and lay on the table. I thought of Silke laying there in pain and scared, I had to control my emotions, my stomach felt like it had been ripped out through my throat, I could hardly swallow and could barely keep the tears at*

bay. The nurse tried to place a catheter in my forearm but failed and tried again in the back of my hand, a tray of syringes was brought over and the first one injected. Looking at the doctor I said it was painful, is that normal? He smiled but the burning was intense then my head started to swim and I can't remember any more.

I've given the grim reaper chance enough to take me, he's not ready yet. My time is not up. In one way I'm glad, "I don't want to die, but I ain't keen on living either". Keen or not I have to. I have to continue to fight my emotions until I can beat them into submission.

Travelling by bike so many hours, so many miles I've had so many thoughts good and bad. But I've always had to move forward, there is no going backwards, you can turn round to travel the same stretch again and again but you're always moving forward, and always something will be different.

Now I'm different. Ready to start again. Ready to live.

For those who knew about Silke's death, thank you for the support you gave to me, for those that knew nothing thank you for the normality you gave to me.

In loving memory of my friend, partner, lover and wife.

I miss you Babe

**Part 7**

**And so....**

I asked my great grandchildren what they thought about when the words 'old people' were mentioned.

**Joe said:** sitting around, bingo, Zimmer frames, 'granny' mobiles, slippers, knitting.
**Molly thought:** not working, pensions, being given a seat on a bus or train, having grandchildren.
**Sam said:** spill food down front when eating.

Oh I try so hard not to spill food down my front! You see it so many times. Pamela, an ex-work colleague, and I were having lunch in a rather nice restaurant the last time I went to London and yes, you've guessed it, that beautiful silk blouse she was wearing had a stain down the front even before we started to eat!

Terms like 'vulnerable' also come to mind when we think of old age. When Joe, who is 6'4" tall, was doing market research after his 'A' levels he knocked on this guy's door and was immediately invited into the house. The chap was so pleased to have a visitor he offered Joe a cup of tea and asked Joe to sit down whilst he answered the questions. Joe was really shocked by this and told the guy that he shouldn't just let anyone in to his house in case of problems.

I know some people say that it's all very well telling us to do this or that but what if there isn't the money available? I only have a very small pension, plus my old age pension, but most of the things I do are free or nearly free. There are others who will go on about their ill-health. I think it has a lot to do with their attitude. If you feel positive about your life; if you try to see the good things in life even if you are bed ridden; if you are willing to accept help offered to you by friends, family or carers, I am sure you must feel better.

On a Friday, my friends Margaret, Joan, Mary and I always try to meet at our club as we call it. It's actually a day centre run by volunteers. You can do all sorts of things there – on a Monday I do my exercise class and Tuesday afternoon and Thursday evening I go to play bridge. We have our lunch there on a Friday so I don't have to bother to cook when I get home but I go mainly for a chat and to laugh. My grandson calls it the 'local home for the bewildered' which is a bit unkind but we don't mind really because we do go on a bit!

Recently, Margaret asked if we remembered Audrey who we knew during the War. Of course we did – that poor girl got pregnant whilst in the land army and her parents refused to have anything to do with her. Her mother wouldn't even allow her to attend the funeral of her father. She met someone who offered to marry her and to take on her child but her mother said no. She made Audrey wait until she was 21 by which time the child had been adopted.

That's one thing that so many stories about the War have in common - pregnancies or the fear of becoming pregnant. With almost no contraception, and also very often very little knowledge, during the 1940's girls often

## And so....

became pregnant. Even if they were married they had to leave their occupation, whether it was the forces, the civil service or wherever. In fact, I know a woman who is still bitter to this day that she had to leave her job in 1945 in the civil service when she became pregnant even though she was happily married. Going back to work after having a child was not an option.

So many women to this day still keep their dark secret of the child they had out of wedlock; the child they gave away for adoption and even their illegal abortion. It seems to me that young people today have it too easy. They can have sex whenever they want, which may be right in some ways, but with that should go responsibilities.

*"Goodness I sound so old talking like this, but I know from personal experience how difficult it was to wait to have sex until I was married."* I said, and that made everyone laugh and we began to reminisce:

Joan started on *"Do you remember how uncomfortable some of the things we had to wear were? Ladies wore corsets, suspender belts, stockings, stays and were considered a 'hussy' if they didn't.*

*Men had to wear a collar and tie every day. They wore braces to keep their trousers up and also some wore braces to keep their socks up".*

*"And another thing"* Joan went on, *"lots of the clothes were non-washable and often hand-me-downs from other people. People made-do and mended."*

## Memories are made of this

"Do you know that in the sixties Charles even wore a collar and tie to play golf?" I reminded them.

"Where I lived", Mary said, "they didn't get electricity until 1954 just after the end of rationing. We had to do our sewing and reading in the kitchen under a gas light. Until then we also had to heat the water on the range both for the bath and for the washing."

Margaret's eyes popped up as she told us that "My job was to turn the mangle every Monday morning for my mum before going to school so that as much water as possible was removed before the washing was put on the line. If it was a rainy day the washing was hung around the furniture in the house. Washing was always done on a Monday, regardless of anything else. I used to hate the smell of damp washing. Of course, all the washing was done by hand although when we did get electricity we had a 'copper' to heat the water but my sister had to keep stirring the washing in the copper with this horrid pole".

"I think the early sixties were the best time for me" she continued. "Someone invented the Hoover Twin tub washing machine". By the time we could afford one, the mangle was powered by electricity too so it was like seventh heaven not having to turn the mangle by hand."

"Talking of school," Mary said, "do you remember having to drink a little bottle of milk every day?"

"Oh I loved that" said Joan "and then along came 'Maggie Thatcher the milk snatcher' as she became known as she

# And so....

*decided the country needed to economise and stopped our daily milk drink."* And we all giggled again.

*"There were no nursery schools or play groups in my day,"* said Margaret, *"I don't remember what we did, but I do know we started school after our 5$^{th}$ birthday and sat in rows, two to a desk. Apart from break times, I don't think we hardly moved at all except to do PE. Most children in my school didn't have their own plimsolls, as we called them. The teacher handed pairs out at the beginning of the lesson and collected them at the end for the next group. Goodness, people would go mad now if you kept wearing any old person's shoes."*

*"The politically correct lobby hadn't been invented when I was young,"* said Mary. *"Everyone knew what you meant, you didn't have some silly intellectual saying you couldn't say this or that. We certainly didn't mean any offence but we didn't know that the words we used were upsetting someone."*

*"The thing I remember most of all was being cold,"* said Joan. We all agreed. *"We had icicles on the inside and on the outside of the windows and we had so many blankets on our bed you could hardly turn over it was so heavy. I remember my mum used to put my clothes for the next day under the blankets at the end of the bed so they were a little warmer to put on. I used to wait until the last minute to get out of the bed, race to the bathroom where there was a useless single bar electric fire. You had to stand right in front of otherwise you couldn't feel it. A quick wash, got dressed and then I ran downstairs for breakfast where my mother had the gas oven on to warm the kitchen"*

## Memories are made of this

Everyone had finished their lunch and things had been cleared away by the time we had stopped talking. Margaret suggested, over a cup of tea, that we should ask people what they remembered about the so called 'good old days'. Here are a few of them:

We only bathed once a week whether you wanted to or not. There were no showers.
When you went to the shops you waited whilst the assistant cut a piece of butter from a huge slab and weighed it for you. It was the same with sugar and tea which came loose in large bags and boxes.
Buying a bag of broken biscuits for almost nothing and sampling one or two before you got home!
Only the milkman had milk and only the baker had bread.
Almost no-one had a fridge until the sixties so food was hung up outside in a ventilated box called a 'safe'
The coalman delivered the coal in sacks which were poured into a bunker or cellar.
Everyone seemed to be superstitious – people were frightened of storms, crossed knives, they touched wood, wearing green was forbidden in some houses. One person said that their gran and mum used to climb in the coal bunker for protection if there was thunder and lightening.
Hardly anyone had a telephone; there were red phone boxes in some streets for the public to use and blue boxes where you could call the police. If you couldn't be contacted easily then a telegram was sent which was delivered by a boy on a bike.
Not many people had cars so people walked, bussed or rode their bikes everywhere

## And so....

For me the most amazing thing was the introduction of the television in the early fifties. Before that, people hardly knew what went on in the next street but soon they knew what was happening across the world!

Oh how things have changed! People often talk about the good old days but there were lots of things that were not so good. People in their 70's and 80's keep talking about the War. I know some people find it boring but for so many it was a life changing experience. What really gets me though is some of these old soldiers who keep going on about what they did during the War. Many of them think the country owes them something. I always feel like saying, 'Get a life'. It's the same as when old people say that young people should respect them. I don't believe that at all. No-one should be respected just because of their age or any other facet of their life. Everyone must earn respect. When I hear old people moaning at our club I feel like having a real go at them but then I think they must be really sad old folk with nothing better to do and then I feel sorry for them.

The other thing old people seem to go on about is how much better life was before – before what I am not sure – but they keep going on about 'life not being the same'. You only get out of life what you put into it so if you are always moaning you will most probably be miserable and say you have a miserable life but if you are positive and look on the bright side of life then life can be fun even in old age!

As we get older we do change, we are probably less tolerant than we used to be; we have higher expectations of others; our attitudes change as do our priorities as to what is important and what is not. We also probably have more knowledge than previous generations. We do have more time available to us but it shouldn't be wasted. We should keep busy, help others and volunteer in any way we can; that way we will not be a burden on friends and family around us. Live life to the full I say; keep fit; be active for as long as you can – even if you can't move about, wave your arms in the air; try to see the funny side of life; laugh a lot!

One thing I am sure about is that I am going to keep fighting in order to avoid being put into a home. I want to remain independent for as long as possible but if I did go into one of those places eventually, I would make sure I wasn't 'drugged up to the eyeballs'

**EPILOGUE from the author**

Old age is the pinnacle of life. It is often very difficult for people to understand as the aging process happens gradually but the essential you doesn't change.

We should, perhaps, slow down a little and enjoy it; not just the present but all our past experiences and memories too. Old people need to be honest with themselves. Of course there will be regrets but focussing on the positive can have a life changing effect.

'That woman is so old she can be any age she wants to be' I heard someone say. It's not just 'wants to be' but 'is allowed to be'. Excuses for, and by, old people are many and various. Don't deny old age, enjoy it! Walk slower, eat and drink more slowly, take time to wash and dress, visit friends/family, enjoy every single day as though it might be your last. After all, does it really matter if you don't have a balanced diet every day or fresh air and exercise? How much will your life expectancy decrease if you don't?

It is to do with quality of life. If you are comfortable and warm; if you care for, and about, others; if you care for yourself; if you make your own decisions about your medication, where you will live and what you wish to happen on your death, then your end of life time can be a very happy and enjoyable time.

Ann Wheal has been a teacher, a university researcher and lecturer. She has published both academic and practical books on children and families including the Foster Carer's Handbook which has sold many thousands of copies. Since her retirement she has published two books in the Scrapbook of World War II Memories series which entailed meeting over 100 people who, during the War, had either been children or who had been in non-conflict occupations, such as nurses, land army and air raid patrol wardens. The stories these people told about their lives inspired Ann to write this book.